HE RAISED A PALE HAND . . .

Until then the October sunlight had been streaming in
through the windows of Miss Eells's office; now the
windows went dark. The two electric lamps in the room
burned yellow and dim and then went out, and a sickly
greenish light, like a halo, appeared. It hovered about the
dark, menacing shape of the stranger. Miss Eells and
Anthony were unable to move. They found that it was hard
to breathe, and they knew that they were helpless in the
presence of someone or something that was unutterably
evil. Evil, and not of this world.

"I will not tell you now who I am," he said. "For the
moment I will tell you only this: I need the book that you
have stolen. Now, I will ask you once more, and once
only: *Did you steal the diary?*"

"FAST, WITTY AND INTRICATE ENTERTAINMENT."
—*Publishers Weekly*

THE
DARK SECRET
OF WEATHEREND

JOHN BELLAIRS

Frontispiece
by Edward Gorey

A BANTAM SKYLARK BOOK®
NEW YORK · TORONTO · LONDON · SYDNEY · AUCKLAND

RL 6, 008–012

THE DARK SECRET OF WEATHEREND
A Bantam Skylark Book / published by arrangement with
Dial Books for Young Readers

PRINTING HISTORY
Dial edition published June 1984
Bantam edition / March 1986

ISBN 0-553-15621-7

Published simultaneously in the United States and Canada

Bantam Books are published by Bantam Books, a division of Bantam Doubleday
Dell Publishing Group, Inc. Its trademark, consisting of the words "Bantam Books"
and the portrayal of a rooster, is Registered in U.S. Patent and Trademark Office and
in other countries. Marca Registrada. Bantam Books, 666 Fifth Avenue, New York,
New York 10103.

PRINTED IN THE UNITED STATES OF AMERICA

CW   13   12   11   10   9   8   7   6

For Toby,
a good editor and a good friend

*The Dark Secret of
Weatherend*

CHAPTER ONE

On a hilly winding road in rural Minnesota, a boy named Anthony Monday was pedaling furiously on a bicycle. The year was 1954, and it was August, and it was broiling hot. Anthony was fourteen years old, with a thin, pinched face, and a long pointed nose. He was tall, skinny, and muscular, and today he was wearing cutoff jeans and sneakers and an old soiled white T-shirt. He was also wearing a red leather cap with a scrunched peak. Anthony had a thing about red leather caps. He wore them summer and winter, in good weather and bad. And when one wore out, he got another exactly like it and scrunched the peak until it looked right. Anthony was going out to see his best friend, an elderly lady named Miss Eells. They had met one day in a drugstore in Hoosac, the industrial town on the Mississippi River where Anthony lived, and they had gotten to be friends in a hurry. Now Anthony had an after-school job as a page at the Hoosac Public Library, which he had gotten through Miss Eells, who was the head librarian. Anthony liked Miss Eells because she was fun to be around. They played chess and Scrabble and went places together. Also Miss Eells listened to Anthony. He could tell her his troubles and his secrets and know that she would not blab about him to anybody else. On this particular day, however, he was not burdened with any secrets that needed to be told. He was just going out to see Miss Eells for fun. She was working at a branch library in the tiny town of Rolling Stone, which was three miles from Hoosac. But three miles is not far to go when you are young and strong, and Anthony was whizzing along at a pretty good clip. Bits of gravel snapped from under his bike's tires as he went, making a sound like popcorn popping. On Anthony rode, legs pumping, singing a song.

Meanwhile, out in Rolling Stone, Miss Eells was in a rotten mood. She was on the lawn behind the little library building, swinging a golf club. It was a nine iron, and she swung it viciously and wildly. As she flailed away, clods of grassy earth flew into the air. The lawn was full of holes where Miss Eells had dug divots, and it was hard to tell whether she was trying to hit the celluloid practice ball or just trying to destroy the lawn. Miss Eells was a small, birdlike woman with a wild nest of white hair on her head. She was sixty-eight years old and wore glasses, but behind them her bright eyes were lively and inquisitive. Normally she was cheerful, but right now she was angry, frustrated, and bored because she was stuck managing the branch library for the summer in this tiny hick town where nothing ever happened. It was true that the library building was quite charming. It was made of red brick and was only one story high, with green shutters and flower boxes under the windows. But all the charming buildings in the world would not have made Miss Eells feel any better about Rolling Stone.

So why was she out here instead of in Hoosac, where she wanted to be? Well, it was all Mrs. Oxenstern's fault.

Mrs. Hanson Oxenstern was the head of the Library Board and a very important person in the city of Hoosac. Miss Eells had never been friendly with Mrs. Oxenstern, but for a long time she had tried to fight down her dislike of the other woman. Then one day Mrs. Oxenstern decided that it would be nice to turn the Children's Room on the second floor of the library into a Genealogy Room. Genealogy is the study of family trees and ancestors, and it can be fascinating if you like that sort of thing. Miss Eells felt that Genealogy was about as interesting and important as bottle cap collecting. A long and bitter argument ensued, in which Miss Eells told Mrs. Oxenstern that she was a stupid, pompous busybody who liked to throw her weight around. Mrs. Oxenstern was furious. She stormed out of Miss Eells's office and slammed the door behind her. Mrs. Oxenstern was pretty powerful, and she would have fired Miss Eells if she could have. But luckily Miss Eells had been at the Hoosac Library for a long time, and she had tenure. All Mrs. Oxenstern could do was force Miss Eells to fill in at the branch libraries around Hoosac if there was an emergency. Of course one day just such an emergency arose. It was the beginning of the summer and old Mrs. Trombly of the Rolling Stone branch was so sick she had to be hospitalized. In no time Mrs. Oxenstern had happily sent Miss Eells over to take her place. So here Miss Eells was, bored silly and angry a lot of the time.

Miss Eells stopped swinging the golf club and looked around. She felt ashamed of herself. Normally she was not the destructive type—not intentionally, anyway. She was kind of clumsy, and she was always spilling things or knocking vases off tables. But she tried hard to be tidy. Now, as she looked around, she realized that she had been taking out her anger and frustration on the lawn. Sighing, she threw down the club and walked around to the front of the library. She felt sweaty, so she took a handkerchief out of the pocket of her skirt and wiped her face. Then she folded her arms and looked around in a discontented way. The library stood at a place where two country roads crossed. Off to the left, at the top of a low bank, was the Spanish-American War monument: a tall granite shaft with some names on it, and two grim old black cannons. Across the street was a variety store, and next to it stood a dignified white frame house with four tall brick chimneys. It was a very picturesque scene, but there was not a soul stirring anywhere. It was three in the afternoon, and there was nobody—absolutely nobody—at the library but Miss Eells. She was so bored that she felt like crying. *Oh, please, God, let something happen soon!* she said to herself. And then—as if in answer to her prayer—around the corner in a cloud of dust came Anthony.

"Anthony! Anthony! Hi! How are you?" Calling out and waving like a madwoman, Miss Eells ran pell-mell across the grass. Anthony swerved his bike off the road. He coasted along the driveway for a short distance, and then he hit the brakes, vaulted nimbly to the ground, and walked his bike the rest of the way to where Miss Eells was standing.

"Hi, Miss Eells!" he said, grinning cheerfully. "I had the day off today, so I thought I'd come out and see you. How're you doin', huh?"

Miss Eells made a sour face. "Don't ask! Actually, if you want to know, I'm bored out of my ever-loving mind! About three people a day come in to use this stupid little library, plus one or two tourists who need to use the bathroom. Thank God you stopped by! I think that in another hour I would have been pitching rocks at passing cars. Come on inside, and I'll get you a Coke."

Anthony followed Miss Eells into the tiny library. It was hot and stuffy inside, even though all the windows were open. A small fan was whirring noisily on top of a filing cabinet, but it didn't seem to help much. There were only two rooms here: a long one full of books on steel shelves, and the disorderly little office where Miss Eells's desk was. Books and papers were strewn everywhere, and there were Coke stains and tea stains and coffee stains all over—on the desk blotter, on the papers, on the floors, and even on the walls. Miss Eells had had a few accidents.

"Welcome to the hermit's cave," said Miss Eells sourly. She swept dust off a chair with her hand and told Anthony to sit down. Then she went over into a dark corner where a small, ancient refrigerator was humming quietly. She opened it, took out two bottles of Coke, and brought them over to the drainboard of a built-in sink that stood by the window. Humming pleasantly, Miss Eells reached into a drawer, took out a bottle opener, and started to pry the cap off one of the Coke bottles. Suddenly she let out a bloodcurdling yelp. The opener clattered to the drainboard. Clutching at her injured hand, Miss Eells rushed past Anthony and made a beeline for the bathroom. The bathroom door slammed, and from behind it Anthony heard the sound of running water. A few minutes later Miss Eells came back. On the index finger of her right hand was a bloodstained Band-Aid.

"There are certain things," she said with a despairing sigh, "which were not meant to be, Anthony. We were not meant to have ice-cold Coke today. So why don't we climb into my car and take a drive in the country? It'll cool us off, and then we can get *really* cool by having an ice cream at the Blue Moon ice cream stand down in Dresbach. How does that grab you?"

Anthony said that it sounded like a good idea. He went outside to lock up his bike behind the library. When he walked back around front he found Miss Eells sitting in her fourteen-year-old Dodge with the motor idling. The car was mud-spattered and covered with rust spots, and it had a bent coat hanger for a radio antenna. Miss Eells had driven it over 204,000 miles, but since it still started every morning, she saw no reason to buy a new one.

"Okay, now," said Miss Eells, waving cheerfully from the open car window. "Let's make ourselves scarce! The library isn't supposed to close for another hour, so if any of Mrs. Oxenstern's spies are hiding in the drainpipes or in the tall grass, I guess I've had it. But at this point I could care less. Come on! Move it or lose it, as my father used to say!"

Anthony climbed in, and they were off. For miles and miles they drove along winding, rutty, bumpy back roads. The air that rushed in through the open windows was like an evening breeze off the sea. As they cruised along, Anthony tilted his head back, eyes closed, and said "Aaah!" several times. Miss Eells began to whistle. She was a great whistler, and she did a medley of songs that had been popular in the forties, like *Racing with the Moon, The Victory Polka,* and *Mairzie Doats.* Uphill and downhill, over a railroad grade crossing and through a sleepy country town, they went. Anthony felt very relaxed—he even took off his red leather cap and let the air whip through his matted, sweaty hair. Soon he was drifting off into a pleasant afternoon snooze, until the car slowed down and rolled to a halt.

Anthony blinked and sat up. He looked around. They had pulled off onto the sandy shoulder of a two-lane blacktop that wound among steep hills. On their right the ground fell away. Anthony saw a long, sloping pasture where cows were lazily munching grass. On the left a saggy wire fence ran along the roadside. Beyond it a fairly steep hill rose up to the skyline. Atop the hill stood a gray stone building with pinnacles on the roof. Anthony was bewildered and annoyed. Why on earth had Miss Eells stopped here?

He turned to look at her. She sat with her hands on the steering wheel, gazing dreamily up at the building on the hill.

"I bet you're wondering why we've stopped," she said without turning. "Well, I wanted to show you Weatherend. That's the name of that estate up there. It's all done in fake Gothic, with fancy pointed arches and pinnacles and ball-flowers. There are fountains and funny court-yards with statues on columns, and I would give my left ear to own the place. It's totally deserted now. Nobody's lived in it for the last forty years. What do you think? Hmmm?"

Anthony didn't know. His head was still full of cob-webs. All around them the landscape dreamed in the simmering heat of the August afternoon. Now that the car had stopped, Anthony was beginning to feel sticky and uncomfortable. Rivulets of sweat were running down his back. What was there to look at? Some old run-down building on a hill? Anthony wanted to get moving again, so they could get to the ice cream stand before it closed.

"Yeah, it's nice," he muttered, and he threw a bored glance toward the far-off gray building. He wanted to add "Let's hit the road, okay?" but he knew that would not be very polite. Tensely he waited for Miss Eells to start the car again.

But she didn't. As Anthony watched curiously she opened the car door and leaped nimbly out. Quickly Miss Eells trotted across the road and stopped in front of the sagging fence, which had two large red No Trespassing signs attached to it. Then she darted back, jumped into the car again, and took off her shoes. As Anthony watched, dumbfounded, Miss Eells reached into the backseat and came up with a pair of white sweat socks and two battered tennis shoes. She slipped the socks on over her nylons and then started pulling on the tennis shoes.

Anthony couldn't stand this any longer. At last he spoke. "Miss Eells," he said in an impatient voice, "what the heck is going on? Are you gonna go on a hike or something?"

Miss Eells grinned and leered at Anthony. "Correction! *We* are going on a hike! Unless of course you want to sit in the car and fester."

Anthony felt helpless. He knew Miss Eells pretty well.

She could be klutzy, she could be vague, she could seem helpless and dithery, but when she really wanted to do something, she was like a runaway locomotive. He felt that he'd better go along. In any case it would be better than waiting in the boiling-hot car.

So Anthony and Miss Eells climbed out and crossed the road. Anthony thought about the No Trespassing signs, and he almost laughed. He had been on hikes with Miss Eells in the past, and he knew that signs like that were like a red cape waved in front of a bull. He had even seen her tear one down once and trample on it. Miss Eells had funny views on a lot of subjects, and on the subject of private property she was practically a socialist.

Miss Eells swung herself quickly over the fence, and Anthony followed. They started up the hill, but as they climbed, Anthony could feel cold fear creeping over his body. What if there were stray dogs lurking? At one time Anthony had liked dogs. If some mutt came ambling up to him, he would pet it and rub its muzzle. But then Anthony had a strange and frightening experience. A stray came after him late one night, barking furiously. Anthony panicked. He started running, tripped over a stone, and broke his arm. Now whenever he was in a lonely place, day or night, an unreasonable fear of dogs would steal over him. In his mind's eye he would see the evil beasts leaping up out of unexpected places, snarling and yelping, with bared fangs and saliva dripping from their mouths. Anthony began to glance nervously to his right and to his left. He was ashamed of his fear and fought against it, but he couldn't do anything to make it go away.

On they climbed. Now they were at the top of the hill. The building that they had seen from the road turned out to be a gray Gothic garage. It was like a miniature church, with quatrefoils and buttresses and narrow pointed windows. In the distance, on a hill that was a little higher than the one they were standing on, loomed the mansion of Weatherend. It was Gothic too, with a gray stone tower and a rose window and knobby, pointed decorations everywhere. But the windows were boarded, and the stone urns that stood on the terrace had been turned upside down. Everywhere the grass was long, rank, and full of weeds. Down in the shallow valley between the two hills Anthony could see a flight of cracked stone steps leading up to a neglected overgrown garden. Two headless sphinxes guarded the top of the stairs, and there were broken marble statues, overturned mossy benches, and weeds galore.

Miss Eells waved her arm at the scene. "See? Isn't this interesting? Wasn't it worth the climb, even in this filthy heat?"

Anthony nodded. He thought the place looked like the setting for a murder mystery. Anthony was reading mysteries now: John Dickson Carr and Agatha Christie and Sir Arthur Conan Doyle. If this were a murder mystery now, he thought, there would be a body down in that garden. Somebody with his head bashed in, or a knife in his back. But life wasn't like mystery novels. There weren't any bodies. There was just the heat and the buzzing of flies and the feeling of loneliness that you get from looking at abandoned houses.

Finally Anthony broke the silence. "Who lived here, Miss Eells? He must've been pretty rich, don't you think?"

"Pretty rich, and pretty weird," agreed Miss Eells. "J. K. Borkman made his money from mining in the Iron Range up north of here, and when he settled down in this place at the age of seventy-two, he decided that he wanted to do two things: First he wanted to live the rest of his life in splendid isolation. Second he wanted to study the weather."

Anthony was startled. "The *weather*?"

Miss Eells nodded firmly. "The weather. I know it sounds ridiculous, but some people are like that. I had an aunt who was nutty about the weather. She would check the weather reports in the newspapers twice a day, and she was always listening to the weather news on the radio. Well, Borkman was just the same. He filled his house with barometers and barographs and thermometers, and there was one of those whirly-cup things on the roof that measured wind speed. And if you ask me why old Borkman had this nutty obsession, I'd have to say that I don't know. In my aunt's case it was probably just something to do to keep from going bananas with boredom." Miss Eells sighed and gazed around. "It's a shame somebody doesn't buy this place and do something

) 14 (

with it. You'd think the National Trust for Historical Preservation would be interested in it, but they aren't. And there aren't many millionaires who want to live in rural Minnesota. So the old place just sits and rots. I've come up here a few times to prowl, and I've never seen a soul. What do you suppose is in this rather pretentious garage, eh? Shall we have a peek?"

Anthony turned and looked at the stout, nail-studded wooden doors of the garage. He saw two twisty wrought-iron door handles held together by a chain that was fastened with a large and very rusty padlock. "But the door's locked," he said.

"I wonder if that's true," said Miss Eells thoughtfully. As Anthony watched, Miss Eells walked up to the door and yanked at the padlock. Flakes of rust showered down, and the lock sprang open. Grinning mischievously, Miss Eells removed the padlock. She threw it contemptuously into the weeds, and with a grand flourish whipped off the chain. Unfortunately the flourish was a bit too dramatic, and the end of the chain whirled around and hit Miss Eells on the back of her neck.

"Ow!" she yelled. "Why me, I ask? Why do these things happen to me?" She sighed and looked down at the chain in her hand. "Ah, well," she said wearily, "it's probably just a judgment on me because I'm a nosy old bat. Come on, Anthony. Let's see what's inside."

And with that, Miss Eells dropped the chain and tugged at one of the garage doors. Anthony grabbed the other door handle and pulled. With a dismal groaning sound the doors shuddered open. In addition to the shut-up, musty smell that drifted out there was an odd, clammy chill to the air, even on this hot day. Inside everything was thickly coated with dust and dirt, and cobwebs festooned the grimy windows. It was so dark that it took Anthony's eyes a few seconds to get used to it. Gradually, though, he began to see things. Flowerpots were stacked in one corner, and nearby were old garden-ing tools, rakes and hoes, and a hand-powered lawn mower. There was a sagging table with more flowerpots on it, plus some trowels and a pair of stiff, dirty garden-ing gloves.

At the back of the building, in the shadows, four large shapes loomed.

Anthony was startled, and afraid. "Hey, Miss Eells!" he said, pointing, "What the heck are those things?"

Miss Eells shrugged. "Darned if I know. Why don't we go find out?" And she walked boldly forward.

At first Anthony hung back. Then he pulled himself together and followed Miss Eells. The boards of the garage floor creaked as he moved cautiously forward. Now he could see what the four things were. Each one looked like a statue that the sculptor had given up on halfway through. From the rugged, chisel-marked stone slabs, hands and arms and bits of carved drapery pro-truded. Half-finished faces, blurred and indistinct and somehow sinister, stared out of the gloom. Oddly enough, the pedestal at the bottom of each statue was finished, squared off, and even polished. On each of the four bases letters stood out in relief. The statues had titles—WIND, SNOW, HAIL, and LIGHTNING.

Miss Eells folded her arms and stared for a full minute at the statues. Then she shook her head slowly and let out a long, low whistle. "Boy, oh, boy!" she said in an awestruck tone. "Would you look at *these*! If you didn't already think that J. K. Borkman was a major fruitcake, with citron chunks and almonds, this would convince you! This is incredible, Anthony, isn't it? What on *earth* do you think the old so-and-so had in mind?"

"I dunno, Miss Eells." Anthony's voice was small and frightened. The feeling of nervousness that had crept up on him since he entered the garage was growing now. There was something about the four half-made statues that was incredibly ominous and forbidding.

Anthony took a sudden step backward. Quickly his hand shot out, and he grabbed Miss Eells's arm. "C'mon," he said. "Let's get outa this place. It's givin' me the creeps!"

Miss Eells stared curiously at the boy. If the statues were sending out evil vibrations, she certainly did not feel them. "Anthony, Anthony, calm *down*!" she exclaimed in an annoyed voice, and she shook off his clutching hand. "Good heavens, but you're nervous today. Does your mother let you drink coffee now?"

Anthony felt foolish. Here he was, a bundle of nerves, and Miss Eells was as steady as a rock. Why wasn't she feeling what he was feeling?

"I . . . I just wanna go," he said in a small, miserable voice. "I can't explain it, but I've just kinda . . . got the heebie-jeebies. You know what I mean?"

Miss Eells smiled sympathetically. She had her own little fusses and worries, and she knew they didn't make sense to anyone but herself. On the other hand she was still feeling nosy and wanted to hang around just a few minutes more.

"We'll go in a couple of seconds," she said, giving Anthony a reassuring pat on the arm. "I just want to have another wee little peek at these statues. They're really quite—ow! Oooh, ow, ow, *ow!*"

Miss Eells had been moving forward as she talked. Suddenly she stumbled and slumped downward. Anthony saw instantly what had happened: a rotten board in the floor of the garage had given way. Miss Eells's right leg had sunk in all the way up to the thigh, and the ragged edge of the broken board had raked her flesh.

In a flash Anthony was down on his knees alongside her. "Oh, my gosh, Miss Eells!" He gasped. "Are you all right? Are you all right?"

Miss Eells bit her lip. Then she opened her mouth and let fly with a string of rather imaginative swear words. When she felt somewhat better, slowly and carefully she began to ease her injured leg up out of the hole.

"Dratted board!" she muttered, and she reached down and broke off the piece of wood that had gouged her leg. She and Anthony looked through the hole she had just made. Even though the light in the garage was dim, they could see, down on the hard ground under the floor, a small metal box.

"Huh!" snorted Miss Eells, and she reached down into the hole and came up with the box in her hands.

"What is it?" asked Anthony eagerly. He was a coin collector, and he was hoping that it was a box full of Brasher doubloons or 1822 five-dollar gold pieces.

"Here," she said, and she handed the box to Anthony. It felt disappointingly light. While Anthony was wondering whether he ought to open it or not, Miss Eells got to her feet and began brushing her skirt with her hands. She winced because of the pain in her leg, and there were long, angry red scrapes on her skin. Her nylon stocking had been ripped to shreds.

"I think I'd better go have Doc Luescher look at this, before tetanus sets in," said Miss Eells wryly, staring down at her injured leg. "Why me?" She sighed. "As I've said many times before, *why me?* Ah, well. Let's get going."

Limping slightly and still wincing from the pain, Miss Eells made her way out of the garage. Anthony followed with the box in his hands. When he stepped into the sunlight, he heaved a sigh of relief—they were safe now. They were going on to the ice cream stand and then home. Anthony turned to Miss Eells, and he was about to ask her if she needed help getting down the hill, when he heard something.

There was a noise in the distance, a door slamming.

Anthony turned and looked off toward the boarded-up mansion. The front door was open, and there was somebody standing out on the front steps. The figure was far away, but it looked like a man, and he was waving. He seemed cheerful and friendly, and Anthony was just raising his arm to wave back when he saw something that filled him with horror.

A dog. A large black dog rushed past the man and bounded down the steps of the terrace. It was coming toward them.

Anthony and Miss Eells turned and ran, lickety-split, down the slope as fast as they could. Injured leg or not, Miss Eells was running hard. She threw it into high gear and passed Anthony, arms pumping like a marathon runner. Anthony was so astounded at the sight of Miss Eells running that he actually slowed down a bit, and so he had the chance to see her hike up her skirts and clear the bent fence in a lovely running jump. With the box still clutched to his chest Anthony vaulted the fence too, and they both scrambled madly across the road. Judging from the sound of the barking behind them, the dog was not very far away.

As Anthony tore around the front of the car he saw out of the corner of his eye that the evil black dog had made it to the fence. He fumbled madly with the door and finally got it open. *Slam*—now he was safe! Miss Eells was inside too, and she was searching madly in her junk-filled handbag for the keys. As she started the car Anthony saw the terrifying sight of the dog leaping viciously at the driver's door. His claws clattered on the glass, and his barking was loud and frightening. Miss Eells turned her head and stuck out her tongue at the yelping beast. Then she threw the car into gear and they shot off in a cloud of exhaust smoke.

CHAPTER TWO

After the frightening experience that they had just had, Miss Eells and Anthony didn't feel much like ice cream. So after barreling along down the road for three or four miles, Miss Eells stopped and made a U-turn, and they went roaring back the way they had come. As they passed the Weatherend estate Anthony noticed that the dog was no longer there. On they went, full speed, until they were back at the Rolling Stone branch library again. Miss Eells nosed the car into a parking space, turned off the motor, and heaved a deep, disgusted sigh. "Well, my friend," she said dryly, "we had ourselves quite a little adventure, didn't we? Only it turned kind of sour at the end. Can you imagine the *nerve* of that creep? Waving at us as if we were long-lost friends and then turning the Hound of the Baskervilles loose on us! Whoever he is, I hope he and his dog both catch the mange and spend the next six weeks scratching themselves silly." She smiled at Anthony. "Ah, well," she added gently, "we did get away, didn't we? I'm really sorry that I dragged you up to that place. I had no idea that anything like *that* would happen!"

"It's okay, Miss Eells," said Anthony. "You didn't know there was anybody up there. Who do you think that guy was, anyway?"

Miss Eells shrugged. "I haven't the faintest idea. Maybe the old dump has a new owner after all these years. But come on—let's go have some ice water and wash our faces and hands. And we'd better call your mom and tell her that you'll be home in a little bit. I'll drive you back." In a lower voice Miss Eells added, "Don't forget to bring that box with you. After all the trouble we went through to get it, I'm dying to see what's inside. It may be old Borkman's laundry lists, but . . . well, who knows? It might just be more interesting."

Miss Eells and Anthony got out of the car and went into the library. They washed up, and Miss Eells peeled off her shredded stocking and threw it away. Then, dabbing gingerly at her leg with a wet washcloth, she cleaned the cuts and put Mercurochrome on them while Anthony took two Coke bottles out of the refrigerator, filled a couple of tall glasses with ice cubes, and poured refreshing drinks for himself and Miss Eells. While they were resting they occasionally glanced at the metal box that Anthony had pulled out of the hole in the floor, which was lying between them on the desk now. It was dented and covered with grime, and it certainly didn't look very much like a treasure chest.

Miss Eells took a long drink of Coke and sat back. "Didn't think I could run like that, did you?" she said, grinning. "Well, I'll have you know that I used to run in the Hoosac Women's Cross-Country race, until the year when I stepped on a sewer grate and sprained my ankle. By the way, when are you going to open up that stupid box?"

Anthony put down his Coke glass and pulled the box toward him. He pried at the lid, and it opened immediately. Inside was a small book with a limp black pebble-grained cover. It looked like a prayer book. When he flipped open the front cover, Anthony saw these words:

The Testament of J. K. Borkman,
or
A Disquisition Concerning the
Inwardness of Things,
and
How the World May Be Altered
And the Clouds Made to Do Your Bidding

Quickly Anthony flipped the page. He saw more handwriting, all neat and orderly, running from the top to the bottom of the blue-ruled leaf. The writing said:

Incense and offerings before the throne of the Most
High, and seven candles lit to the seven thrones of
knowledge, and the four thrones of the bringers of
lightning, hail, wind, and snow. How I will laugh,
when I have brought low those who mocked me!
Jupiter the Hurler of Bolts stands again in the
temple. A roaring wind shall sweep aside Unbeliever
and Fool, and the slate will be wiped clean, so that
life may begin anew. . . .

Anthony stopped reading. With a puzzled frown on his face he reached across the desk and handed the book to Miss Eells. She flipped back to the title page, and then quickly scanned the lines that Anthony had read. Miss Eells turned a page, and another. She arched her eyebrows and wrinkled up her nose, as if she were smelling Limburger cheese. Finally she heaved a big sigh and tossed the book down onto the desk.

"Lord love a duck!" she exclaimed. "I have never read such insane bibble-babble in my life! I hope that old Borkman had fun doing this, because I'd hate to think he was *serious*! And who do you suppose this Pam character is? An old girl friend, maybe?"

Anthony was thoroughly bewildered. He had only read the first page, so he didn't know what Miss Eells was talking about. "Huh? Who's Pam?"

Miss Eells reached out and picked up the book again. She flipped to the middle and held the page up so Anthony could see it. Across one whole sheet, in straggling letters, was written the name *PAM*. Then

Miss Eells turned to another page. The letters were almost as big here, and the message read:

PAM UNDER THE CRACK OF NOON

Miss Eells turned some more pages. She held up the book once again and showed Anthony some more words, scrawled diagonally across two whole leaves this time:

Question: Does the sonorous bus go ____-____?

Miss Eells pitched the book onto the desk. She shook her head slowly and frowned. "That sure does take the burnt cookie!" she muttered. "I knew old J.K. was dotty, but I guess I didn't realize quite *how* dotty he was!" Miss Eells laughed suddenly. "Hah! I wonder if Mrs. Oxenstern would like this book for our library? She could put it in the Rare Book Room—I'm sure it's the only one of its kind in existence!"

Anthony didn't laugh. He just looked pouty and stared at the desk. He had hoped they'd found a real treasure, not just junk. Why couldn't the box have contained a letter by William Shakespeare? He had read somewhere that a genuine Shakespeare letter would be worth a million and a half dollars, if anyone ever came up with one. This crummy book was worth about three cents. And for that they had nearly gotten eaten alive!

Miss Eells glanced at her watch and announced it was

time to go. Anthony got up. He stared dejectedly at the objects on the desk.

"Whaddaya think I ought to do with these, Miss Eells?" he asked, pointing.

Miss Eells shrugged. "Suit yourself. If I were you, though, I'd pitch the box and save the book. Who knows? Some day a notebook kept by the famous eccentric J. K. Borkman may be worth some money."

Anthony took Miss Eells's advice. After throwing the box in a wastebasket and tucking the book under his arm, he helped Miss Eells turn out the lights and lock up the library. Anthony went out behind the building and got his bike. He put it in the trunk of Miss Eells's car and tied the trunk lid down with some old bicycle inner tubes that Miss Eells carried around with her.

As they sped away Miss Eells and Anthony did not notice the black Packard that came rolling up out of the leafy hollow behind the library. It slowed down and halted as it drew near the crossroads, and for several minutes it just sat with its motor idling. Then the car turned right and headed on up the road toward Hoosac.

The rest of August passed uneventfully. Mrs. Trombly got better and went back to her job at the Rolling Stone library, and Miss Eells happily returned to her job in Hoosac. September came, and Anthony started as a freshman at Hoosac High School. And amid all the hurry and confusion of the new school year, he quickly forgot about the strange adventure that he and his eccentric friend had had.

One chilly evening in the middle of September, Anthony was sitting at one of the long tables in the East Reading Room of the Hoosac library. He had finished shelving books, and now he was trying to catch up on his homework. Except for Miss Eells and himself the library was empty. She was sitting at the main desk and reading the Hoosac *Daily Sentinel*. Suddenly she let out a loud exclamation.

"Good heavens!"

Anthony looked up. He was startled to hear loud talking in the library. "Huh? What is it?"

Miss Eells beckoned to Anthony. "Come over here, my friend, and you'll see. It has to do with the little incident we were involved in last month. Weird things are going on around Hoosac."

Anthony got up and walked over to the desk. Miss Eells had the paper spread out flat in front of her, and with her forefinger she tapped a headline that read OLD ESTATE TO BE RENOVATED. Above the story was a photo, and with a shock Anthony recognized the place where it had been taken: it was the weedy, overgrown garden at the Weatherend estate! But the garden looked different now. The bushes had been pruned, and the overturned stone benches had been set back in place. The broken statues had been repaired, and heads had been put on the two stone sphinxes that crouched at the top of the staircase.

"My gosh, Miss Eells," exclaimed Anthony. "Somebody's fixing the old place up!"

"Yes, my friend, somebody certainly is," she replied, and she gave Anthony a strange, unreadable look. "Well, go on. Read the article underneath. It's fascinating, in a way."

Anthony looked down at the story that went with the picture and read:

> Lovers of architecture and historical preservationists will be delighted to learn that the estate of Weatherend, on the Winona Post Road six miles south of Rolling Stone, is going to spring to life again. It has recently been revealed that A. Anders Borkman, the son of J. K. Borkman, has returned from a lengthy stay in Norway and will take up residence in the house that his father built. Mr. Borkman plans to completely restore and renovate the mansion and its grounds. He is independently wealthy and a collector of antique statues and other art objects. When Weatherend has been restored to its former grandeur, Mr. Borkman plans to organize guided tours and is also slated to give lectures on architecture and sculpture at Immaculate Conception Academy. Those in the Hoosac area who remember the elder Mr. Borkman will be interested to know that his son has brought back to the estate the collection of barometers and other meteorological instruments. . . .

Anthony stopped reading. He turned to Miss Eells with a frown on his face. "My gosh!" he said. "Do you think that's the guy who waved at us before he turned his dog loose?"

Miss Eells took off her glasses and rubbed at the bridge of her nose with her fingers. "Could be. Or it might have been one of his pals—if he has any. This whole business really amazes me. I can't imagine that J. K. Borkman had a wife and son. It's . . . well, it's sort of like Dracula settling down to be a restaurant owner in Cedar Rapids, Iowa. It's very, very unlikely. But the son is here, and he seems—God help us—to be following in his dear old daddy's footsteps. You'd think he could find something better to do with his time than to imitate that old creep."

Again Anthony looked at the photograph. An odd thought had occurred to him. "Do . . . do you think he'll do anything with those statues that we found in the garage?"

Miss Eells smiled wryly. "Oh, he'll probably set them up in some place of honor. For all I know, they may be wonderful examples of modern sculpture. Ah, well. Let's leave Mr. Borkman and his unfriendly dog and his crazy statues. There are other weird things going on in the Upper Mississippi Valley." She turned the page. "Did you know that there has been a rash of break-ins lately? In Catholic churches?"

Anthony stared. He hadn't heard about this.

"Mm-hmm," Miss Eells went on, nodding. "And do you know what they've been stealing? The *altar stones!*"

Again Anthony stared. His folks didn't go to church, so "altar stones" meant nothing to him.

Miss Eells laughed. "Ah, I can see you didn't grow up in a Catholic household like I did! In the center of the altar in a Catholic church there is usually a flat stone with five little red crosses cut into it. Under each cross a relic is buried. Relics are pieces of the bones of saints, like a chip off of Saint Anthony's shinbone or a chunk of Saint Agnes's skull. Why anyone would want to swipe an altar stone is beyond me. Maybe it's somebody who hates Catholics or who thinks the relics will bring him good luck. And . . ."

Miss Eells's voice trailed off. She sat up straight in her chair, listening.

Anthony glanced this way and that. "What is it? What's wrong?"

And then he heard it. A rattling noise. Something was clattering against the windows of the library.

"Hail!" said Miss Eells suddenly. "It's hail!" She jumped up and ran into the East Reading Room, with Anthony right behind her. Grabbing the metal handles on one window sash, Miss Eells tugged. The window opened, and Anthony saw little white bits of ice jumping on the stone ledge. In a flash he thought of the craggy unfinished statue with the word *Hail* on its base. And for no particular reason, he felt afraid.

Toward the end of September there was another hailstorm, but it was much wilder and stranger than the first one. Out in the countryside around Hoosac hailstones the size of golf balls were reported. They dented the hoods and roofs of cars and killed chickens in hen yards. A few people got caught out in the open when the storm hit, and they were bruised and badly frightened by the big balls of ice. With the hail came lightning—lots of it, sizzling blue and red and white bolts. Trees were set on fire, and lightning rods on the roofs of barns and houses melted. In one farmhouse a glowing blue ball of electricity rolled up the front steps, ripped the screen from the front door, and wadded it into a smoldering mass of half-melted metal. Wild winds uprooted trees and flung them across roads, and loud peals of thunder boomed and reverberated in the hills. Even the older people in the area could not remember a storm that was quite so violent or bizarre. Then came the tornadoes. On October 5 a violent electrical storm hit the Hoosac area. There were high winds, and at least five tornadoes were sighted. One of them roared through a graveyard near La Crosse and gouged deep, raw gashes in the earth. It reopened old graves and threw rotten coffin wood and bones all over the cemetery. And again there was vivid colored lightning, with red and blue fireballs rolling down roads and across fields.

In the city of Hoosac there was something like a panic. Frightened people kept calling up the Police Department,

City Hall, and the Weather Bureau. Some were convinced that atomic testing had thrown the world's weather out of whack. Others said that God was angry at the world because of its sinfulness. But most were simply worried and upset. At the Hoosac Public Library all the talk was about the weather. Miss Pratt, the assistant librarian, was firmly convinced that sunspots were the cause of it all. Other people had their own ideas, and they argued a lot about who was right. However, as the days passed, and the weather returned to normal, the talk and the panic died down. People decided that their worries were foolish, and they began to fuss about other things.

Anthony Monday had his own ideas about the strange weather and what was causing it. These ideas took shape in his head over a period of several days, and when it suddenly occurred to him what nonsense it was, he almost laughed. But then he thought some more, and he began to wonder if maybe there was something to his odd thoughts after all. One evening, when he and his parents were sitting in the living room watching television, he decided that he would bring the subject up. Nervously he glanced at the two people who were sitting in the darkness near him. How would they react to his strange notions? He had a pretty good idea of what his mother would say: she was a sarcastic, skeptical kind of person, and she would probably doubt him. Anthony decided that he would rather talk to his dad alone.

Patiently Anthony waited for the right moment. At

last the phone rang, and Mrs. Monday got up to answer it. She went out to the front hall, and presently Anthony heard her pulling the sliding door shut. Great! It was probably one of her friends, and they would be yakking for hours.

When a commercial came on Anthony cleared his throat. "Uh . . . Dad?"

Mr. Monday was a placid, potbellied man. He ran a saloon, and normally, on a weekday evening like this one, he would have been hard at work. But his hired bartender was running the place tonight, and Mr. Monday was taking a well-deserved night off. He was in a good mood.

"Yeah, what is it, Tony?"

"Uh, well, whaddaya think about all the weird weather we've been havin'?"

Mr. Monday shrugged. "I dunno. I don't really understand about that kinda stuff, but anyways I'm glad it's over. I betcha the atomic bombs had somethin' to do with it, though. The government don't tell us a darned thing about what they're doin', but someday it'll all come out, you mark my words." He shifted uneasily in his chair.

Anthony coughed again. He was having trouble finding words for what he wanted to say. "But, Dad," he said in a strained voice, "what . . . I mean, what if somebody could use, like, magic to . . . kind of make bad weather happen? I read in a story once where a witch—"

Mr. Monday snorted. "*Witch?* Good God, Tony, is that the kinda stuff they're teachin' you down at the high school? Nobody believes in witches anymore! Are you kiddin' me or what?"

Anthony wanted to say something more, but the commercial was over, the program was coming on again, and he knew his dad hated to be interrupted while he was watching something good. So that was the end of that.

One day later that week Anthony was on his way home from the library when he decided that he would stop in at the garage on Second Avenue where his brother worked and pay him a little visit. Keith was eighteen, and he was in love with cars. He worked as a mechanic, and he was always covered with grease and surrounded by a litter of spare auto parts. When Anthony walked in, Keith was standing under a car that was up on a lift. He was wearing his dirty coveralls, and he was banging at something with a hammer. Glancing over at Anthony, he stopped, wiped his hands, and stepped forward with a friendly grin.

"Hi, kid!" he said, waving. "So what brings you down to this joint? You lookin' for another spare-time job?"

Anthony glanced away. He felt uncomfortable. His brother was a very matter-of-fact, hardheaded sort. Also he'd made it clear that he thought Anthony was gullible. How could he bring up what he wanted to talk about?

"I . . . I just wondered how you were," said Anthony. Then, after an awkward pause, he rushed on. "It's . . . it's nice to have the weather back to normal, isn't it? Those . . . those hailstorms and stuff were kinda hard to take, weren't they?"

Keith stared at his brother curiously. The two of them had discussed the strange weather before. Like everyone else in Hoosac, they had chewed the topic over during lunchtime and dinnertime conversations. So why was Anthony bringing it up now?

"Well, it's over with, anyway," said Keith with a bored shrug and a little half-grin. "So did you come all the way down here to ask me what I thought about the weather?"

Anthony's mind was racing. He had to find some way to make this conversation seem sensible. "We . . . we were talkin' about it in school," he said, staring hard at a puddle of oil on the floor. "And one kid said that . . . that maybe somebody was usin' magic to make the hail and lightning happen. Whaddaya think of that?"

Keith did a double take, and then he burst into loud laughter. "Somebody said *that*? *Jeez!* They must've had rocks in their head! I bet it was that Lothamar kid—you know, the one with the stuffed-up nose? His mom's a Holy Roller, and they believe all kinds of junk like that."

Anthony could feel his ears getting hot. He forced himself to smile, and he even managed a little laugh. "Naw, it . . . it wasn't him. It was somebody else. Well, I hafta go home and help Mom with somethin'. See ya 'round."

And with that, Anthony turned abruptly and walked out of the garage, leaving his brother to stare after him with a puzzled frown on his face.

On down the street Anthony stalked. He felt angry,

frustrated, and humiliated. Why had he ever tried to shove his theories off onto his brother or his father? He ought to have known what the result would be. They were both real no-nonsense, down-to-earth types. They thought that anyone who believed in magic was crazy. Even though Anthony couldn't prove his theories, he knew he was right. He had to tell somebody, or he would burst. And then it hit him—of *course*! He could tell Miss Eells! She was his best friend, and the only person in all the world who really listened to him. He always went to her with his secrets. And she never laughed at his notions even when she disagreed with him.

And so, every evening for a week, Anthony went off to work at the library, thinking, *Tonight I'm gonna tell Miss Eells about my ideas.* But each time he choked up, figuring, *Naw, she'll laugh at me too.* Finally, on a rainy Sunday evening, he decided that he could not keep silent any longer. After dinner he went up to his room, opened a drawer in his desk, and took out the mildewed book that was full of the mad ravings of old J. K. Borkman. And with the book under his arm and an umbrella held over his head, he set out for Miss Eells's house.

As he came tramping up the long walk that led to Miss Eells's front door Anthony heard music, squawky and out-of-tune. It came drifting out through an open window—even in October Miss Eells was a fresh-air fiend, and she had windows open all over the house. As he listened to the terrible noise Anthony grinned. He had heard Miss Eells playing her parlor organ before. A parlor organ is an instrument that, even when played well, sounded like a muffled accordion. Miss Eells did not play well. Not that she minded much—she only played to amuse herself.

Anthony rang the doorbell. The noise stopped, and in a few seconds Miss Eells opened the door. She was wearing a quilted blue robe, pajamas, and slippers. A pencil was stuck into the bun of gray hair on her head.

"Hi, Anthony!" she said cheerfully. "What brings you out on this rotten night?"

Anthony put down his umbrella and shook it. He eyed Miss Eells nervously. "Can . . . can I come in?"

Miss Eells laughed. "No, you have to stand out there and let water run down your face. Of *course* you can come in! Don't act so timid and apologetic—you've known me longer than that, for heaven's sake! And what's that you've got under your arm, eh?"

Anthony blushed. "It's . . . it's that book we found out at the old estate. That's what I want to talk to you about."

Miss Eells was surprised, but she said nothing. Anthony stepped in and propped his umbrella in the corner. He hung his dripping raincoat up on the coat tree and followed Miss Eells out to the kitchen. She turned on the flame under the teakettle, and when the water was hot, she made two big mugs of instant cocoa. Then the two of them went into the living room to talk.

Miss Eells settled herself in an easy chair and sipped

her cocoa. Anthony was on the couch, with the book propped awkwardly on his knees, trying to figure out where to begin.

"Now, then," said Miss Eells, smiling pleasantly. "What is all this? Have you found the riddle of the universe imbedded in the mad bibble-babble of old J. K. Borkman?"

Anthony squirmed. He wished that Miss Eells wouldn't make fun of him. After taking a noisy slurp of cocoa he set the mug down on the coffee table and picked up the book. It was stuck full of paper bookmarks that he had used to mark passages he thought were important.

"You . . . you know all this weird weather we've been having?" he began.

Miss Eells looked at Anthony strangely. "Yes . . . yes, I am aware that we have been having peculiar weather lately. What about it?"

Anthony took a deep breath. He opened the book to one of the places that he had marked. "Just listen to this," he said, and he started to read. " 'The world is a filthy and defiled place. Human life is made ugly and unbearable by sickness, war, cruelty, and stupidity. If only all could be made clean again! What if whirlwinds and fires from heaven, tempests and floods and rains, were to wash clean the earth so that life might begin anew? If the slate were wiped clean, the new writing might be fairer than the old. And with the aid of the Four Servants, the gods of tempest and howling gale, the unimaginable deed might be done! Elsewhere in these pages I have set down the method by which the deed may be accomplished. But still I am afraid, mightily afraid to begin this thing. Is it right to do this? Would good come from such utter devastation? I cannot do it myself. Let one who comes after me set the wheels in motion. Would that I might live to see this New Earth that is to come! *Earth might be fair, and all men glad and wise* . . . that is what the hymn says, and those words may yet come true. . . .' "

Anthony's voice trailed off. He laid the book down and gave Miss Eells a long, meaningful look. "Well?" he said. "Doncha see? Doesn't this explain what's been goin' on lately?"

Miss Eells looked utterly mystified. She gazed off into space for a second . . . and then it hit her. "Oh!" she said, and her hand shot up to her mouth. "Oh, good grief! You mean you think—" The corners of her mouth began to quiver. She wanted to laugh, but she didn't want to hurt Anthony's feelings. Her face went through several contortions, and then she faked a sneeze and blew her nose into her hanky. Finally she felt that she had regained control of herself and could answer him.

"I hate to be critical, Anthony," began Miss Eells in a grave, exceptionally calm voice, "but I really think you're going off the deep end on this one. I know that we have been having some pretty unusual weather lately, but to connect that with the four statues we saw in Borkman's garage or with the apocalyptic drivel he wrote down in that book there . . . no. No indeed, my friend. You're making a big fat hairy mistake. People can't control the weather with magic—it's just not possible. I mean, we can seed the clouds and make rain, but that is about the only way that human beings can have even a teeny-weeny little bit of control over the weather. For all our fancy technology we are still pretty darned helpless when Mother Nature cuts loose. No, my boy— forget about this, please. It's just your imagination working overtime."

Anthony was crushed. He had been so sure that Miss Eells would believe his theory. His dad and his brother might shoot down his grand notions, but he had expected some understanding from his old and trusted friend. He stared forlornly at the book on his lap. Then he started to get up.

"I'm sorry I wasted your time," he said glumly as he turned to go. "I'll get my coat and—"

"Oh, Anthony, for heaven's sake, *sit down!*" As she said this Miss Eells leaped to her feet and accidentally spilled her cocoa. It fell with a *splop!* on the floor, but Miss Eells just looked at the stain spreading on the rug and laughed out loud. She stood there cackling with the mug still in her hand while a jingle she had learned years ago ran through her head:

> Hasten, Jason, bring the basin!
> Oop, slop! Bring the mop!

Anthony was still standing by the couch glowering. Then he relaxed and grinned. As he stood by, watching, Miss Eells went out to the kitchen. She came back with a wet washcloth, knelt down, and began to scrub at the stain on the rug. As she scrubbed she talked.

"You see, my friend? My clumsiness has its good points after all. You would have stormed on out of here if I hadn't spilled this stuff. But now we're good friends again—at least I hope we are." Miss Eells stopped scrubbing and looked up. She saw that Anthony was still smiling, and this reassured her. "Look, Tony," she said gently, "I didn't mean to rain on your parade. Your theory is no more far out than some of the stuff that wise, respectable people say on the TV or in the newspapers. But your idea just doesn't make it. Sure, we've had some insane weather lately, but nature is full of peculiar happenings. The storms'll blow over, and life will go on, as boring and predictable as ever. You'll see."

Anthony *didn't* see, but he also didn't feel like arguing anymore. So he shrugged his shoulders and asked Miss Eells if she would like to play a game of Scrabble. She was delighted. Miss Eells was an avid Scrabble player, and she played for blood. Out came the old battered set, and the two of them went happily out to the dining room table to play. Meanwhile the rain rattled against the windows, and the wind moaned down the chimney of the living room fireplace. It was a dreary sound, but a perfectly natural one. As he arranged the letter tiles on the rack in front of him Anthony told himself that Miss Eells was probably right.

All the same, he was scared. And the fear would not go away.

CHAPTER THREE

As the end of October drew near, the Hoosac Public Library began getting ready for the opening of the Genealogy Room. Miss Eells was looking forward to this event about as much as the average person looks forward to an attack of the flu. The big day had been set for October 29. In the privacy of her office Miss Eells sourly confided to Anthony that the ceremony ought to be a Halloween party, with Mrs. Oxenstern coming as the Goodyear blimp. Miss Eells was still quite bitter about the Genealogy Room, and she was even angrier about the fact that she would have to be present at the opening ceremony and the reception afterward. But as head librarian she could hardly stay away. And so she grimly began to prepare herself to say nice things to everyone, even to Mrs. Oxenstern.

On the day of the opening ceremony Anthony came to work at the library as usual. He arrived around three thirty in the afternoon, and as he walked in the front door he saw a man standing at the main desk talking to Miss Eells. He was about medium height and wore an expensive-looking coat over a pin-striped suit. Drawing close, Anthony was able to get a good look at his face, and what he saw was not pleasant. Above a well-trimmed black beard the man's cheeks were sunken, and there were dark circles around his eyes. The curve of his full red lips made it look as if he were about to say something very cruel or very sarcastic.

"Hi, Miss Eells!" said Anthony. He waved cheerfully at his friend and cast a nervous glance at the strange man.

Miss Eells turned and gave Anthony a hard, meaningful stare. In a strained, tense voice she said, "Anthony, this is Mr. Anders Borkman. He's the gentleman who owns the Weatherend estate out near Rolling Stone. He's come to apply for a library card."

Anthony's mouth dropped open. Was he the one who had waved pleasantly while he had turned the dog loose on them? Maybe so—he sure looked mean enough. And if he was the one, did he recognize Anthony and Miss Eells as the two trespassers he had chased away?

Mr. Borkman smiled coldly and held out a long, pale hand. "How do you do, young man," he said in a flat, toneless voice.

Anthony hesitated a second, and then reached out to shake hands. Mr. Borkman's hand felt lifeless and surprisingly cold. But the man's stare was hard and hostile. It hit Anthony like a slap in the face, and in that instant he thought, *He knows who we are. He knows us both, and he hates us.*

Mr. Borkman withdrew his hand from Anthony's grasp and thrust it into his overcoat pocket. He turned back to Miss Eells. "Now, then," he said in a crisp, businesslike tone, "do you have all the information you need?"

Miss Eells looked at the white card on the desk in front of her. "Yes," she said, nodding. "I think this will be sufficient. There'll be some delay while we process this, but you ought to get your card by—"

Mr. Borkman cut her off. "The delay is unimportant to me. But if we have finished with this I would like to talk to you and this young gentleman in the privacy of your office."

Miss Eells had been writing something on the card, but now she laid down her pen and looked up. Her eyes were wide with fear. Normally she would have said "Sorry, some other time." But there was a command in Borkman's voice, and when Miss Eells's eyes met his, she felt a numbing shock. Suddenly she envisioned four rugged stones standing on a grassy hilltop. The grass was long and rank, and behind it was a dark, stormy sky. When the picture faded, Miss Eells found she had no will of her own. She had to do whatever Anders Borkman asked.

"All right," she said dully, and she dragged herself to her feet. Anthony felt confused and frightened. Why didn't Miss Eells tell this creep off and make him go away? But as he was about to open his mouth to protest, Borkman turned his gaze upon him. Suddenly he felt the same sensation Miss Eells had. It was as if there were an invisible electrical field around this sinister-looking man that surged out and enveloped him. It numbed him and made him unable to resist. Moving woodenly, he followed Miss Eells and Borkman through the tiny reference room and down the long, narrow corridor that led to Miss Eells's office.

Miss Eells paused to unlock the heavy paneled door, then the three of them filed in. The door closed softly, and Miss Eells and Anthony shuffled across the room like a couple of windup metal soldiers. Stiffly Miss Eells sat down behind her cluttered desk. Anthony sank into a slouchy leather armchair, and Borkman carried a tall stool that was standing against a wall out to the center of the room and sat down on it. He looked from one to the other with an air of haughty authority. He would be making all the big speeches while Miss Eells and Anthony would just sit, glassy-eyed, as if they had been drugged.

Borkman folded his arms across his chest. He stared at a point on the wall above Miss Eells's head, and he began speaking in a calm, measured voice.

"I have been observing you for some time. Trespassers need to be watched—you are dangerous, lawless types. But I have no wish to prosecute you." Borkman coughed.

"You took a diary in a metal box from the carriage house of my estate. My father told me of its existence, but he neglected to mention where he had hidden it. Recently, when I was in the carriage house, I found a hole in the floor and saw a square indentation in the earth underneath. It occurred to me that the diary must have been removed from that spot—by you. Am I correct?"

Miss Eells and Anthony sat as still as statues. Neither of them moved a muscle.

Borkman glared coldly at the two of them. "I shall ask you both again," he said in a harsh, menacing voice. "But first I see that you need further persuasion."

He raised a pale hand. Until then the October sunlight had been streaming in through the windows of Miss Eells's office; now the windows went dark. The two electric lamps in the room burned yellow and dim and then went out, and a sickly greenish light, like a halo, appeared. It hovered about the dark, menacing shape of Anders Borkman. Miss Eells and Anthony were still unable to move. They found that it was hard to breathe, and yet their minds were clear—horribly clear. They knew that they were helpless in the presence of someone or something that was unutterably evil. Evil, and not of this world.

"I will not tell you now who I am," said Borkman in a voice that echoed oddly, "but there will be a time in the future when you will know me better. For the moment I will tell you only this: I need the book that you have stolen so that I may complete the great work that my father began. You find it hard to breathe, do you not? Well, I can make it harder. I can cause torments of the mind and body that you never believed possible. So I will ask you once more, and once only, before I show you a worse side of myself: *Did you steal the book?*"

Miss Eells nodded. So did Anthony.

Borkman grinned evilly. "I thought so. Which of you has the book now?"

Miss Eells remained silent and motionless. But in a slow, dreamy voice, as if he were talking in his sleep, Anthony spoke: "I have the book. It's in my room at home."

Borkman turned toward him. His face was a scarcely human mask of grinning malice. "Is that where it is?" he crooned. "Well, then, my fine burglarious friend, I have a small request to make. Tomorrow night at midnight I want you to bring me the book. I'll be on the front steps of the Hoosac City Hall. And you'd better do as I say, or else you and this old woman here will suffer. And I mean *suffer*. Do I make myself clear?"

Anthony answered haltingly. "I'll bring . . . the book to you. Don't . . . don't hurt Miss Eells. Please don't."

Borkman's evil smile broadened. "Oh, don't worry. Your friend will remain unharmed if you fulfill your part of the bargain. And now I must go. But I command you both, and I order you by the Sign of the Four and the God of Storms! *Neither of you will remember this conversation or anything that has just transpired in this room. You, Anthony, will do what you have promised, but you will not know why you are doing it. So be it, so be it. Amen.*"

Borkman clapped his hands. The darkness drained away. The lamps came on, and sunlight streamed into the room. And there they were, the three of them sitting in their places and looking as if they had just finished a very pleasant conversation.

Nimbly Borkman sprang down off the stool. He shook hands quickly—first with Anthony, then with Miss Eells. "It's been very pleasant to make your acquaintance," he said smoothly. "And now I must be going. I can expect that library card in a week or so, can I? Good. Have a pleasant afternoon." And with that, Anders Borkman swept out of the room and closed the door behind him.

For a few seconds neither Anthony nor Miss Eells moved. Then Anthony shook himself and blinked. He felt a bit confused but generally cheerful.

"Gee, Miss Eells," he said, smiling vaguely, "that Anders Borkman is kind of a nice guy after all, isn't he?"

Miss Eells leaned forward and rested her arms on the desk. She folded and unfolded her hands and stared hard at the green marble penholder. "I guess so," she said in a faraway, abstracted voice. She looked troubled and seemed to be on the point of saying something. But instead she shook her head, sighed, and got to her feet.

"I've got work to do," she muttered as she headed for the door. "There are eight zillion things that have to be done before the big wingding tonight. And you had better get back to work too. I'll see you later."

Anthony went out into the library stacks, and for the next hour he trundled the book cart up and down the aisles putting books back in place. Every now and then, though, he would stop in the middle of what he was doing and try to figure out what was wrong inside his head. *Something* was out of whack, that was for sure. It was as if there was a blank space, something he couldn't account for. But then he would laugh and tell himself that he was being silly and go on shelving books.

The party that evening in the Genealogy Room went very well. Miss Eells was there in a stunning blue silk dress and a pearl necklace. The dress was a bit on the dramatic side, but Miss Eells felt good in it, and needed the boost to help her through the whole stupid affair. Anthony was there in a busboy outfit, handing out cups of punch to people and carrying around trays of hors d'oeuvres and cookies. Sometimes he would run into Miss Eells and they would both smile and make little jokes. And then—for no reason—they would both frown in a puzzled way. They knew something was wrong, but they didn't know what.

The next day, Saturday, was sunny and unusually warm. Anthony played a game of touch football with friends in the afternoon, and later he saw a movie. When he went to bed that night, he felt the very odd sensation that he had something to do. This was idiotic, and he knew it. Tomorrow was Sunday, another free day. Oh, well, thought Anthony, Miss Eells always says that people get funny ideas at bedtime because the human machine is worn down then and needs rest. Feeling slightly relieved, he yawned, turned out the light, and went to bed.

At half past eleven the Monday house was dark and silent. A full moon threw pale silvery streaks across the floor of Anthony's bedroom. Anthony stirred and got up, padding across the room to his desk. He took something out of the desk drawer and went to the chair where his clothes were laid out. Soon he was dressed. He picked up the diary, tucked it under his arm, and left the room, closing the door softly behind him.

A short while later Anthony was standing on the steps of City Hall. The huge old building, a fortress of black stone, cast its shadow over him and hid him from sight. Across the street the illuminated clock in the tower of the Methodist church said it was one minute to twelve. A cold night wind sent leaves scuttering across the street. Anthony stood dead still, waiting. And as the clock began to toll midnight a car came crawling around the corner. With a soft purring sound it crept along the curb and stopped in front of City Hall. One of the car's doors opened, and Anthony walked slowly and stiffly down the steps, heading for the car. He paused by the opened door as a hand reached out and took the diary from him. The door closed, and with a sudden accelerating roar the car sped away. Anthony stood staring after it for a full minute, and then he turned and walked down the street back into the silent darkness.

CHAPTER FOUR

When Anthony woke up the next morning, he felt as if he had been hit on the head with a hammer. Woozily he turned his head and looked at the clock on his bedside table. It was five minutes after ten! Luckily it was Sunday, and there wasn't anything crucial that he had to do that morning. Anthony sat up and peeled back the covers. He swung his legs out of bed and looked down, and then he got a shock. He was wearing his socks! How in the heck had *that* happened? Anthony never wore his socks to bed. Curious, he turned and looked at the chair that stood at the foot of his bed. He always draped his shirt and pants neatly over the chair if he was going to wear them the next day, and laid out tomorrow's underwear and socks on top of the pants. But the chair was bare, and his clothes lay scattered over the bedroom floor. Anthony was frightened. He thought about the blank feeling he had had yesterday, and he became even more upset. What was going on?

Anthony went down the hall to the bathroom. He splashed water on his face and brushed his teeth. As he was rinsing his mouth he thought about the book full of J. K. Borkman's mad ravings and about meeting his son Anders. Maybe there was a curse on the book. Maybe that was why his mind had been playing tricks on him lately. Well, if that was the case, he ought to just take the book out and burn it in the incinerator in the back-yard. Anthony walked back to his bedroom. Carefully he began to open the bottom left-hand drawer of his desk. Inch by inch he slid it out, as if he expected the book to spew flames in his face. A little more . . .

And then he got his third shock of the morning. The book was gone!

Anthony stepped back. His mouth dropped open, and he could feel the palms of his hands getting sweaty. Then all of a sudden he got angry. His *mother*! Had she been messing around in his desk and swiped the book? Anthony's mother was a bit on the nosy side. She found it hard to keep out of his business, and once or twice she had even opened mail that had been sent to him. For the time being all worries about these mysterious goings-on were swept out of Anthony's mind. His mother had no right to go poking around in his desk, and Anthony would go downstairs and tell her so.

Mrs. Monday was sitting at the kitchen table, cutting up carrots for the big Sunday dinner. She was not a pleasant-looking person. Her mouth was always set in a thin-lipped, suspicious frown. She could be kind, but she had a sour attitude toward the world in general.

Anthony burst into the room, filled with righteous anger. "Mom!" he said in a loud, accusing voice. "Did you take a book out of my desk?"

Mrs. Monday laid down the paring knife. At first she looked utterly stunned, but then she got angry. "No!" she said in a voice that was just as loud as his. "No, I did *not* take anything from your desk, and I'll thank you not to go around making wild accusations. I try hard to respect your privacy, and I wouldn't *dream* of prying into your personal affairs." Mrs. Monday paused. "What sort of a book was it?" she asked.

Anthony was about to answer, but he hesitated. He didn't want his mom to find out about their expedition to the Weatherend estate. He shrugged carelessly. "Oh, uh, it . . . it was just a crummy old book with a leather cover. It was somebody's diary, I guess. I, uh, found it in a barn."

"I see. Well, as I said, I have not been muxing about in your desk, and I haven't seen any book of that description anywhere in this house. And now, I'd like to go back to fixing dinner!"

Anthony stared gloomily at his mother. He knew from her tone that she didn't have the diary. If she did, she would have been evasive, but there was only anger in her voice now. So then what *had* happened to the blasted book? Had he been walking in his sleep last night? Had he taken the diary away himself while he was in a trance? But he had never walked in his sleep before. It was all very, very strange.

"I'm sorry, Mom," he said at last. "I shouldn't've flown off the handle like that." Anthony smiled weakly at his mother. He wanted to smooth things over a bit so she wouldn't be mad at him about his "accusation." "Is . . . is there anything I can do to help?" he asked timidly.

Mrs. Monday smiled up at her son. "You bet your life there is," she said. "You can help me peel some potatoes!"

One sunny morning later that week Miss Eells was up in the tower room of the library, sorting magazines. She was wearing a blue denim apron, and an old-fashioned turk's-head feather duster lay at her side. Miss Eells was kneeling down, and she was reading a thrilling story in the June 1951 issue of *Cosmopolitan*. That was the trouble with sorting magazines. You just had to stop every now and then to look at something fascinating. Oh, well, it was better to do this than to think about what was going on at four o'clock that afternoon. Miss Eells groaned. Mrs. Oxenstern was throwing yet another sweet little tea party up in the new Genealogy Room. It was enough to make you sick. First the grand opening party, and now a tea for the Minnesota Genealogical Society. And who was expected to be there, all dressed up and looking sweet and saying nice, polite, boring things? Why, Miss Eells, the head librarian, of course.

Miss Eells ground her teeth and sighed. Then she got up, brushed dust off her apron, and looked around in dismay at the tall, tottering piles of old, dog-eared magazines and journals. *I have to get organized,* she said to herself. At that moment a blast of wind hit the tower, making the loose glass in the windows rattle. Gazing wistfully out at the park far below, she thought how badly she wanted to be out there, flying a kite. . . .

Brr-rrr-rrring!

Miss Eells jumped a little and looked up at a small white plastic box mounted over the tower room's only door. Set in one end of the box was a small red warning light. It was blinking on and off, and the box vibrated as the alarm bell rang again. It meant that someone was at the main desk.

Br-rring! The bell rang again. Whoever it was was getting impatient. Miss Eells threw down her feather duster and bustled off toward the stairs.

When she got to the main desk, Miss Eells found none other than Anders Borkman glowering into space. He was holding a briefcase in one hand, and with his other hand he was jabbing the alarm button.

"Good morning, Mr. Borkman," said Miss Eells, and she smiled politely as she seated herself. "I'm sorry there was no one here when you came in."

"So am I," said Borkman snappishly. "I'm rather busy

at present. I have one book to return, and another to renew. And I'd appreciate it if you'd hurry."

And with that Borkman raised the briefcase and deposited it on the desk. With a fussy flourish he undid the clasp and took out two books. One was a large blue tome called *Weather Patterns of the Upper Mississippi Valley*. The other was a small, battered volume with a black oilskin cover. There was no title that Miss Eells could see, but a Dewey decimal number had been printed on the spine in white ink. Borkman told Miss Eells that he wanted to renew the blue volume. The other was simply being returned.

When the blue book had been stamped, Borkman took it and slid it into the briefcase. He nodded stiffly at Miss Eells and started to go.

"Nice day, isn't it?" said Miss Eells pleasantly as she pulled the black book toward her.

"Eh?" said Borkman, staring malevolently at her.

Miss Eells met Borkman's gaze—for some reason she wasn't afraid of him this time. "I *said*, it's a nice day, isn't it?"

Borkman sniffed contemptuously. "It may be, for some. But I prefer turbulent weather—storms and lashing rains and raging seas. I suppose my tastes are odd, but I feel that such weather rouses the spirit within one. It tests one's mettle."

Miss Eells did not say what she thought about this rather pompous little speech. She merely shrugged and began flipping through her desk calendar. As Borkman went out she glanced up at him quickly, and then she shook her head. She had been uncertain about him before, but now her mind was made up. *Test one's mettle, your grandmother!* she muttered under her breath. She hated phony, pretentious people.

Miss Eells pulled the black book toward her and opened the front cover. And then she did a double take; she had never seen this book before. The frontispiece was a dark old woodcut that showed bearded men seated around a large table. The title page was done in Old English type and said

THE
BOOK OF THE DEAD
by
Simon of Salisbury

Quidquid latet, apparebit
Nil inultum remanebit
—Venantius Fortunatus

London, 1873

Well! said Miss Eells to herself. *This is one on me! I thought I knew most of the old books in this library.* She flipped through it quickly, and to her surprise she found that it was all printed in Old English letters and appeared to be written entirely in Latin.

Miss Eells closed the book and frowned. What on earth was this book doing in the library, anyway? Several years ago she had gone through the place thoroughly trying to weed out all the old unreadable books that had just been gathering dust for years. How had this one gotten past her? Miss Eells turned it over in her hands. She wanted to pitch it into the nearest wastebasket, but since it appeared to be a real library book, with a card in the catalogue, she figured she'd better put it back where it belonged. Later she could figure out how to get rid of it officially. With the book in her hand Miss Eells headed back into the stacks. As she went she sidled past a teenager who was standing on a stool, straining to reach a volume on the top rack. She glanced quickly at the long row of green Loeb Classical Library volumes. Again she checked the book's decimal number. . . . Aha! This was the right section. Miss Eells stopped. She saw a gap on one shelf and was about to stuff the black volume into it when something happened.

There was a slight hissing sound, and a puff of bluish dust rose from the top of the book. Like pipe smoke the little dust cloud came twisting and drifting through the air. A sweetish, perfumy smell tickled Miss Eells's nostrils. She felt dazed and a little faint, and suddenly in her mind's eye she saw that ring of standing stones again. Four leaning weathered boulders on a grassy hill and in the background a dark, humpbacked mountain and a stormy sky. Then the vision vanished, and the cloud of sweet-smelling dust was gone. Miss Eells stood there, stunned, with the black book in her hand.

She felt very confused and a bit frightened. Had she been working too hard lately? Overworked and worn-out people sometimes had hallucinations. Maybe she ought to take a couple of aspirin and go lie down for a bit. She stuck the book into the gap on the shelf and hurried away.

Miss Eells stayed in her office for the rest of the morning, and then went out to lunch. When she got back, she felt light-headed and feverish. Maybe she was coming down with a cold. Oh, well, if she was, there wasn't much that could be done about it.

The early afternoon passed in its usual way, and then at a quarter to four Anthony showed up for work. That was late for him, but he had had to stay after school for a play rehearsal. He found Miss Eells standing in front of the fireplace in the East Reading Room. She was staring at herself in the mirror that hung over the mantel, and she was fiddling with loose strands of gray hair that stuck out from her bun-shaped hairdo.

"Oh, hi, Anthony," she said, turning. "I'm getting all gussied up for the shindig that's going on upstairs at four. Don't I look devastating?"

Anthony giggled. "Yeah, you look okay, I guess."

Miss Eells made a face. "I honestly don't know." She sighed. "Sometimes I wonder if I was cut out to be a little old lady. I'm supposed to *like* tea parties, but personally I'd rather be on a slow boat to China. Also I feel kind of out of sorts today. Oh, well. I don't suppose I have to stay *forever*. See you later."

And with that, Miss Eells turned and dragged herself toward the staircase. From the look on her face you would have thought she was going to the dentist to have a wisdom tooth pulled.

A few minutes later Miss Eells stepped into the Genealogy Room. There were ladies galore: tall ones, short ones, fat ones, thin ones. In flower-print dresses, with cameo brooches, lace at the throat, pearl necklaces, and all. On a table near the door stood two silver-plated urns, one with hot water for tea and the other with coffee, and a huge glass punch bowl full of pinkish liquid. Nearby on another table were plates of little triangular sandwiches and bowls of peanuts. At the far end of the room a string quartet was playing. In the midst of all this was Mrs. Oxenstern, bigger than life and twice as bossy-looking. She was wearing her best white silk dress, and on her collar was the jeweled American flag pin that she always wore on special occasions. And, as usual, her silver-gray hair was done in a rippling permanent wave that looked *so* permanent Miss Eells always imagined attacking it with a hammer and chisel to uncover the plaster beneath. Everything was as it should be—polite and proper and indescribably boring.

Miss Eells advanced into the room. She passed up the tea urn and the coffee urn and took a cup of punch. She sipped and winced—it was so sweet that it made her fillings ache. With the cup in her hand she turned and looked this way and that. And at that moment something very strange happened.

It was as if Miss Eells had been suddenly seized by some force outside herself. She went reeling madly across the room, elbowing people aside and slopping punch everywhere. She stopped in front of Mrs. Oxenstern, and then, with a jerky motion of her hand, she threw the punch all over the front of the fat woman's dress. All Mrs. Oxenstern could do was stare in stupefied horror. Miss Eells was shocked too. She tried to speak, but only a strangled sound emerged from her throat. Then the force took hold of her again and flung her back across the room, to the table where the coffee urn was. Picking up two cups of coffee, one in each hand, Miss Eells went charging off. She raced the full length of the room as the bystanders ducked and dodged to get out of her way. She was headed straight toward the large Chinese vase that stood on a pedestal near one of the tall windows—one of Mrs. Oxenstern's prized possessions. Mrs. Oxenstern had lent it to the library because she wanted the Genealogy Room to look spiffy. Everyone was too shocked to move. They all just stood watching in slack-jawed amazement as the head librarian of the Hoosac Public Library went cannoning into the pedestal. The vase rocked, fell, and smashed to smithereens. One cup went flying one way, the other flew another, and Miss Eells fell down on her back, unconscious. The party was over.

CHAPTER FIVE

After the crash an awful silence fell in the room. Everyone stood dead still, staring at the unconscious form of Miss Eells. In the middle of the room stood Mrs. Oxenstern. Across the front of her dress was a large pink stain. Her fists were clenched, her face was very red, and she was trembling all over with fury. When she could finally make herself move, she turned and stalked out of the room, walked down the stairs, and went straight into Miss Eells's office. She picked up the phone and called the police. Then she called the Hoosac *Daily Sentinel*, and, finally, the hospital. When she had finished phoning, Mrs. Oxenstern no longer looked angry—she looked triumphant.

Three days later, on a cold, gusty November evening, Anthony Monday was ringing the doorbell of Miss Eells's house. He felt very bad. Miss Eells had been suspended from her job at the library. Although she hadn't exactly been fired yet, everybody figured that it was only going to be a matter of time before that happened. Wild stories were going around about her. Some people claimed she had been drinking on the day of the awful incident, while others said that she had gone crazy and hinted darkly that there was insanity in Miss Eells's family. Anthony's mother did not like Miss Eells, and so she believed both the drunk and insanity stories, and went around saying that she had "seen this coming" for a long time. As for Anthony himself, he was shocked and saddened by what had happened. At first he had absolutely refused to believe the things he heard about Miss Eells's wild behavior. On the day of the party he had seen her leave the library looking very grim and frightened, and of course he knew from all the commotion that *something* had gone wrong. But when people told him what had occurred, he just couldn't accept it. Then, finally, on the day after the incident, Miss Eells called Anthony up and gave him her version. She told him that something very strange was going on and that perhaps Anders Borkman was behind it all. Anthony responded by telling her of the strange disappearance of Borkman's journal, and Miss Eells suggested that Anthony come over soon, so they could figure out what to do.

And so here he was, in his leather jacket and red

leather cap. Under his arm was a box of Dorfmeier's chocolates, the special dark, soft-centered assortment. Anthony's finger jabbed at the bell button. He pushed it again and again impatiently. All sorts of wild fears had been running through his mind lately. He had heard that people who lost their jobs often flipped out. It was true that Miss Eells had sounded quite level-headed when he talked to her on the phone, but still . . .

There was a rattling sound. A chain was unhooked, a bolt was drawn back. The door opened and there stood Miss Eells, wearing one of her tasteless fake-Japanese kimonos with dragons all over it. Around her waist was a wide fringed sash, and stuck into it was a tiny samurai sword in a wooden sheath. It was a souvenir letter opener that she had gotten once on a trip to Japan. Miss Eells looked pale and drawn, but her eyes were clear and she was smiling.

"Hi, kid!" she said, and she gave Anthony a jaunty little wave. "It's good to see you, and I'm glad you're still speaking to me. Some people aren't, you know."

Tears sprang to Anthony's eyes. "Anyone that won't talk to you is a dumbhead and a creep," he said angrily. "The stuff that happened wasn't your fault. Somebody made you do it." Suddenly Anthony remembered the box of chocolates. "Here," he said, smiling. "This's for you."

Miss Eells was touched. Now there were tears in *her* eyes. "Come on in," she said, giving Anthony a friendly pat on the arm. She smiled wryly as she looked at the candy box. "My, my! Just what I need! I'll be able to get fat while I collect my unemployment checks. Come on in! Don't just stand there with that woebegone look on your face! Let's see what's what, okay?"

A few minutes later Anthony was seated on Miss Eells's saggy couch with a bottle of Coke in his hand. Miss Eells was kneeling in front of the fireplace, toasting English muffins the old-fashioned way because her toaster was broken and she kept forgetting to have it fixed. As Anthony watched she turned the muffin this way and that, trying to get it browned evenly on both sides. Near her on the floor was a big jar of Frank Cooper's Oxford marmalade, a spoon, a couple of butter knives, and a stack of untoasted muffins. They were going to have a feast.

"Whaddaya think about that book disappearing and me waking up with my socks on?" Anthony asked. "What's goin' on?"

Miss Eells pursed up her lips. "Nothing good, that's for sure!" She turned and looked hard at him. "Tony, how come you never told me about the disappearance of Borkman's journal before?"

Anthony hung his head. "I . . . I just didn't wanta talk about it. I was scared that I might be goin' outa my mind."

Miss Eells smiled sympathetically. "Well, you weren't —or if you were, you've got company now. But it doesn't seem terribly likely that we're both going bats at the same time. Remember the day when Anders Borkman came to the library and had a talk with us in my office? Well, I have the darnedest odd feeling about that talk. I can't remember one little tiny thing," she said. "It's as if the whole time we spent in the office has been erased from my mind."

Anthony nodded. "Yeah. It's . . . it's like it was all part of a dream or something like that."

Miss Eells took the muffin off her fork, put it on a plate, and started buttering it. She added a big dollop of marmalade, spreading around with the back of the spoon, and handed the plate to Anthony.

"A dream, eh?" she said thoughtfully as she put another muffin on the fork. "Yes . . . Borkman's visit was a bit like that, I suppose. And then, right afterward, you felt you'd been someplace in the middle of the night, only you couldn't remember where, and then whammo! Old Borkman's journal was gone! And speaking of disappearing books, the weird black book that he returned has totally vanished."

Anthony was startled.

"Yup, it's gone!" Miss Eells said solemnly. "I used my passkey to sneak back into the library the night before last, and there's just a gap on the shelf where I put it. Anthony, I am *sure* the dust Borkman put on that weird book made me do all those strange things at Mrs. Oxenstern's party. And you know what else I'm sure of?"

As Miss Eells turned dramatically, pointing the toasting fork straight at Anthony, she discovered that there was a flaming muffin on the end of it. With a yell she jumped up, shook the muffin off onto the floor, and stomped on it with her foot. That done, she quickly dropped to her knees, picked up the charred muffin gingerly, and flipped it into the fire. But she was too late. There was a big ugly scorch mark on the rug.

Miss Eells looked at Anthony helplessly. Then she laughed silently until the tears were running down her face. "Oh, dear!" she said, shaking her head and dabbing at her eyes with her handkerchief. "What next, Tony? I ask you." Finally getting control of herself, she stood up and brushed crumbs off her kimono. "As I was saying when the Great Fire broke out, I think Anders Borkman is dabbling in sorcery. The idea sounds incredible, I know, but I can't think of any other explanation for the insane things that have been happening to us lately." Miss Eells folded her arms. She turned and gave Anthony a long, searching look. And when she spoke again, there was a genuine tremor of fear in her voice.

"Anthony, I'm worried. If Borkman—young Borkman —is using magic on us then . . . maybe the threats in old Borkman's diary were not just a lot of lunatic nonsense." She paused. "I know, I know! You tried to tell me this before, and I wouldn't listen. But now I think it *is* possible that the son has come back to finish the evil work that his father began. Remember when you read me that passage out of Borkman's diary? Well, there's a phrase that sticks in my mind: *Let one who comes after me set the wheels in motion.* Maybe . . ." Miss Eells's voice trailed off. She looked despondent. "Oh, Lord, ·

Lord!" she exclaimed, shaking her head in despair. "If only he hadn't swiped the diary. Why didn't we have the sense to make a copy?"

Anthony brightened up and grinned. "We did . . . er, I mean, *I* did!" I made one at the library with the new Thermofax machine. I just wanted to see how the machine worked. And—"

He never got to finish his sentence. With a joyous whoop Miss Eells rushed across the room and threw her arms around the boy, knocking his cap off in the process. "You wonderful, bright, clever, charming person!" she crowed delightedly. "You're a genius, you really, truly are! Where is it? Where did you put it? Did you bring it with you?"

As soon as he could get a word in edgewise, Anthony explained that the Thermofax copy of Borkman's diary was tucked away in the bottom of one of his desk drawers at home.

Miss Eells looked worried. "Are you sure it didn't disappear with the original? Have you checked?"

Anthony smiled confidently. "Yeah. It's still there."

Miss Eells heaved a sigh of relief. "Good! Let's hope it stays there till we get a chance to look at it. And now could I ask you to toast another muffin for me? I'll go out in the kitchen and brew a pot of my disgusting Lapsang souchong tea, and then we'll figure out what we ought to do next. Okay?"

Anthony got busy with the toasting fork while Miss Eells went to the kitchen. Soon she returned with her big flowered Staffordshire teapot, steam curling up from the spout. Anthony recognized the smell drifting toward him; it was like a pile of burning wet leaves.

After taking off the lid of the teapot and sniffing the rich, smoky aroma, Miss Eells poured herself a big, brimming cup. Then she settled herself in her wingback chair and took the muffin that Anthony handed her. As she munched and sipped she stared off into space. There was silence in the room.

Suddenly, with a loud, alarming clatter, Miss Eells set down the cup, saucer, and plate. She leaped up, pulled the little samurai sword letter opener out of her belt, and brandished the tiny blade.

"We've got to *attack*!" she exclaimed. "We've got to get him before he gets us!"

Anthony gaped. He wondered if Miss Eells really had gone off her trolley this time. Then she turned, saw the expression on his face, and laughed. Throwing the letter opener down on the coffee table, she smiled sheepishly and said, "I get a bit dramatic sometimes. It comes from my grandfather, who was a Shakespearean actor. What I meant was, we've got to find some way to get inside Borkman's estate. Maybe he's planning to pull some dirty work with those four statues we saw—Wind, Snow, Hail, and Lightning. Something's going on, that's for sure, but we really don't have an awful lot of information yet. If we can find some evidence, maybe we can use that book full of the old man's crackbrained ravings and really skewer him to the wall!" Miss Eells paused and smiled mischievously. "Besides," she added, "snooping around the grounds of the villain's estate always works in the movies."

Anthony did not quite understand the logic of what Miss Eells had said. "How're we gonna break into Mr. Borkman's place?" he asked.

"I don't really know," Miss Eells replied placidly. "But I'm sure I'll think of something. Actually I wasn't planning on *breaking* in. I had something more subtle in mind—" She snapped her fingers. "I know! I'll get hold of my brother, Emerson! He'll know what to do! He always has sneaky, tricky, devious plans and strategies up his sleeve. He can get us into Weatherend—I'd bet money on it!"

Anthony knew Emerson Eells well. Emerson was a lawyer up in St. Cloud. He was a little rabbity man with a big shock of white hair and a very precise way of talking. When Anthony had gone on trial because of a treasure he had found, Emerson had defended him. Anthony liked and respected his courage and resourcefulness, and felt if anyone could get them onto Borkman's estate, he could.

But suddenly an unpleasant thought occurred to Anthony. "Miss Eells," he began, frowning, "what're you gonna do about your job? Are they really gonna fire you?"

Miss Eells stopped smiling. Her jaunty manner vanished, and she suddenly looked old and careworn. She stared at the tea leaves in the bottom of her cup, as if she were trying to read her fortune there. "I honestly don't know what the library board will do, Anthony. For the time being I've been suspended from my job, without pay, and the board will meet again in early December to decide my fate. I will admit that things do not look terribly rosy. After all, I've only got one friend on the board, and that's Mrs. Bump, the reporter who kept the story out of the *Sentinel*. But it's a seven-member board, and you can be sure that Mrs. Oxenstern will hang me from the yardarm if she can possibly manage to do it."

Miss Eells was almost speaking in a whisper. Anthony could hear the fire crackling and the Waterbury clock ticking on the mantel. Suddenly he was filled with righteous anger. They couldn't do this to Miss Eells—they just couldn't! Quickly his anger turned to fear. If Miss Eells was fired, how would she manage to live?

Miss Eells looked at Anthony and smiled wanly.

"Don't worry, kid," she said, chuckling. "I have some money put away, and what with Social Security checks and sponging off my rich brother, I'll survive. But—"

Suddenly there was a loud, reverberating peal of thunder and an instant later a blue flash of lightning leaped through the living room windows. The antique plates on the mantel rattled, and the lights dimmed. Miss Eells looked stunned for a second; then she leaped out of her seat. Motioning for Anthony to follow her, she rushed out into the hall and headed for the front door.

They paused on the front stoop and looked up. The air

was bitterly cold; the sky was clear. Overhead the stars were clustered thickly, and the faint whitish track of the Milky Way visible. In the distance the dark, irregular shadow of the Mississippi bluffs rose against the sky. But all that they could hear was a faint rumble, like the sound of a distant train. Miss Eells and Anthony looked at each other fearfully. Then Miss Eells turned and gazed off toward the faraway line of bluffs. The anxious look on her face had changed to one of grim determination.

"I think we had better get busy," she said quietly. "And I hope to God we are not too late."

CHAPTER SIX

The dreary days of November dragged past. After a brief spell of clear weather the sky became overcast and stayed that way. Cold, drizzling rain fell, and raw, gusty winds blew from every corner of the compass. Anthony didn't enjoy working at the library as much anymore. Miss Pratt, the assistant librarian, was in charge now, and she and Anthony had never gotten along very well. But very often on his way home from the library Anthony stopped to see Miss Eells.

On the first of these visits Anthony brought his copy of old Borkman's journal with him and left it with Miss Eells so she could study it. In turn Miss Eells reported to Anthony that she had talked on the phone with her brother, Emerson. She had finally managed to persuade him that there was a dangerous situation developing in Hoosac. But Emerson needed some time to formulate a plan, and he said he would call her when he was ready.

Two days before Thanksgiving, Anthony got a phone call from Miss Eells. She said that Emerson was at her house. Could Anthony come over for a short while that evening? Breathlessly he answered that yes, of course he'd be over, as soon as he could get away after dinner. Then he hung up and went in to eat with his family. He tried hard to act normal, but his dad and Keith both noticed that he seemed edgy. When Keith asked him what was bothering him, Anthony replied that he was cramming for an algebra test that he had to take early in December. That seemed to settle the matter—at least Anthony hoped that it did.

Later, when Anthony entered Miss Eells's living room, there was Emerson, sitting at the parlor organ. He was wearing an expensive-looking dark wool sweater and blue pin-striped pants, and he was puffing on one of his many antique meerschaum pipes. This one was shaped like a sea nymph who had her arms wrapped around a cornucopia. As soon as he saw Anthony, Emerson grinned. He stopped playing, put his pipe in an ashtray, and bounced to his feet.

"It's good to see you again, Anthony!" he said as he vigorously pumped the boy's hand. "I haven't laid eyes on you since the affair of the Winterborn treasure, and I've been wondering how you were doing. Myra says that you want to become a doctor someday. Is that right?"

Anthony nodded, and he had just opened his mouth to say something, when Emerson cut in.

"Well, I think that's fine. But whatever you do, for heaven's sake don't change your mind and decide to become a *lawyer*! When I was a kid I read bloodcurdling novels about lawyers who became detectives in their spare time, shooting at villains and saving beautiful women from danger. Now that I really am a lawyer, I spend my time reading great, thick, dull books and drawing up wills for elderly misers. I'm so bored that I'll even jump at the chance to take part in one of my sister's hare-brained schemes."

"Thanks a lot, buddy!" said Miss Eells. She was sitting in her wing chair by the fire and sipping crème de menthe from a delicate liqueur glass. "Don't let my dear brother kid you," she went on to Anthony. "If he didn't believe that this whole thing was pretty darned serious, he wouldn't be down here. Would you, Em?"

Emerson's manner changed. He stopped acting devil-may-care and grew very serious. Sitting down on the piano stool, he cocked one leg up on his knee. Then he folded his arms across his chest and scowled at the rug. "I wouldn't, indeed," he said, nodding gravely. "Something has got to be done—no doubt about it. As soon as Myra told me over the phone about the things that had been happening to you two, I knew right away that you had been the victims of a sorcerer."

Emerson glanced up, and when he saw Anthony's astonished expression, he laughed. "Surprised that I know about such bizarre things? Well, I'm not nearly such an old fuddy-duddy as I may seem. Actually, I am interested in magic. I've read a great deal about wizards, and I've delved into their books of spells. I know what they can and can't do, and I can tell when a genuine master of the black arts is at work."

Emerson smoothed his sweater fussily and then took his pipe out of the ashtray and began to turn it over in his hands. Suddenly he shot a piercing glance at Anthony. "We are up against someone who is *very* dangerous," he said, pointing a warning finger. "Unless I miss my guess, Anders Borkman is a cold-blooded fanatic who will stop at nothing to carry out the ghastly plans of his maniac father. According to an article I saw in the newspapers, he's already dragged those four statues out of the garage. There was a picture with the article showing the statues set up in a corner of his estate. Furthermore, I've looked at the copy that you made of old Borkman's crazy journal. Well, it doesn't take too much savvy to figure out what *he* has in mind! He wants to use the weather to wipe the earth as clean as a billiard ball so that the world could start all over, fresh and clean, shiny and new." Emerson grimaced. Then he laughed harshly. "Hah! He's not the first one who's thought that the world would be better if we could all go back to the beginning again! But none of the other crackpots who've had that idea have actually had the ability to turn their dreams into reality." Emerson shuddered. He was thinking of the power that Anders Borkman wielded. Then he looked hard at Anthony again.

"If you decide to be part of our little raiding party," he said solemnly, "there is some risk involved. I wouldn't think you were a coward if you decided not to go along with Myra and me when we take a closer look at Borkman's estate."

Anthony did not flinch, but met Emerson with a steady gaze. "I want to go with you, Mr. Eells," he said quietly.

Emerson Eells smiled warmly. He got up and walked over to Anthony and gave him a good strong squeeze on the arm.

"Good for you, my boy," he said. "Actually, if we manage this thing right, there won't be an *awful* lot of danger. But there's always the unknown factor, and I thought I'd better warn you. Now, then! I think we all ought to adjourn to the dining room. There are some documents and maps that we should be looking at. Myra, would you get Anthony a Coke and bring me a bottle of beer? Maps tax the brain and parch the throat, you know."

A few minutes later Anthony, Miss Eells, and Emerson were all standing around the dining room table looking at a large cracked map that had been spread out in the middle of it. The four corners were held down by three German beer steins and a chunk of roseate quartz. In one corner of the map was a label inside a fancy Victorian engraved border. The label said:

The Country Estate
of
WEATHEREND
Formerly the residence
of the noted industrialist
Jorgen Knut Borkman, Esq.

Near the map was a stack of dark old engravings. The one on top showed a ring of standing stones in a field of long, rank grass. The caption identified the site as *The Weird Sisters, Carmarthenshire, Wales.*

Emerson Eells took a swig from the beer bottle in his hand. Then he gave the picture of the standing stones to Anthony. "Those stones," he said, tapping the edge of the picture with the bottle, "were involved in a case of witchcraft that might be similar to the one we're dealing with. Somebody drilled holes in them and inserted little packets of beeswax wrapped in paper. Imbedded in the wax were clots of human blood, fingernail parings, snippets of hair, and little pieces of bone that—"

"Hey!" said Anthony, interrupting. "I bet it was Borkman that stole all those altar stones from the churches around here! They've got bones in 'em, and—"

"I'm way ahead of you," said Emerson with a superior smile. "Myra told me about the altar stones over the phone earlier, and I'll get to them in good time. But to return to the Carmarthenshire case, the packets were inserted in the stones to set up magical lines of force, influences stronger than the strongest electrical field.

Then, I imagine, some rather picturesque rituals were performed, and incantations were chanted. The result was that certain *things* started to happen."

Anthony had been studying the picture. Now he looked up. "Things?" he said in a puzzled tone. "What kind of things?"

Emerson shrugged carelessly. "That part of Carmarthenshire started having the most wild and woolly weather that anyone can remember. Hail and winds violent enough to blow the roofs off houses. Blizzards in places where there hadn't been any for over four hundred years. And colored lightning and mysterious underground rumblings. People later claimed that the ghosts of dead friends and relatives had been seen wandering the streets and pressing their noses against people's windows in the middle of the night."

Emerson paused. "I mention all this," he went on, "because I think the same sort of thing is going on here. In the case of the Weird Sisters of Carmarthenshire the disturbances stopped after the angry townsfolk tipped over the stones, extracted the little packets, and burned them. Now, here's what we have to do."

Miss Eells and Anthony crowded in close to the table. Taking a pencil that was stuck behind his ear, Emerson pointed at the snaky line that ran up the middle of the map.

"This is the driveway that runs from the entrance of the estate right up to the circular carriage drive outside the front door of the mansion," Emerson said. "Down here, not far from the entrance, is an unused tennis court and some dilapidated buildings that used to contain showers and dressing rooms. There's an old dried-up ornamental fountain too, and—"

"Wait just a minute," said Miss Eells, interrupting. "How come you know so darned much about the Borkman estate? You're giving us information that you could never have gotten from just studying this forty-year-old map."

Emerson smirked. "My dear sister, do you think I spend all my time sitting up in my room in St. Cloud, making cats' cradles with yarn? Do you remember when I came down to visit you early last summer? Well, on my way out of town I stopped by Weatherend to poke around. I had heard about its sinister reputation from some friends of mine, and I was curious. Fortunately young Borkman had not repaired the wall around the estate then, so I was able to sneak in. But back to the business at hand. Near the tennis court and the fountain is a small grove of cedar trees, and inside that are the four statues that we are concerned with. Now, what I propose to do is this. I have an old paneled truck with doors on the back. I'll have it painted so it looks like it's from the Hoosac Gas Company. Then I'll get some gray coveralls, and—"

Once again Miss Eells interrupted. "Oh, come on, Em!" she said, laughing. "You look about as much like a gas man as King Kong. How on earth do you expect to fool Borkman?"

Emerson Eells glowered at his sister. "My dear Myra," he said frostily, "I wasn't aware that gas men came in only one size and shape."

"All right, all right, you're a gas man!" said Miss Eells, shaking her head. "So after you've arrived in your impenetrable disguise, what do you do then?"

"If you'll shut up and listen, I'll tell you," snapped Emerson. With the pencil he tapped the oblong space on the map that was labeled *Tennis Court.* "You two," he went on, "will be hiding in the back of the truck. I'll let you out near the tennis courts, and then you will run and conceal yourselves in the ruined buildings. Then, while I'm up at the mansion distracting Borkman by pretending to read his meter, you'll go skulking over to the grove of cedar trees. Now, understand! I don't want you to do anything fancy. I just want you to examine the four statues and find the holes that—if I'm right—will have been drilled in them. They'll almost certainly be camouflaged in some way. Plugged with gray putty perhaps. And in the holes—if my guesswork is correct—will be little packets of *bones.* From the altar stones that you mentioned earlier, Anthony. Almost certainly, the theft of those bones was Borkman's work. The blessed bones of saints can be used by evil men for evil purposes. But, remember! Don't try digging the packets out of the holes. Just find the holes and mark them with white chalk. Then, when you've done that, skedaddle back to the tennis court and stay out of sight till I come by and pick you up in the truck."

"Are we gonna come back and knock over those stones sometime?" asked Anthony.

Emerson pursed his lips. "My dear Anthony," he said, smiling in his precise and infuriating way, "*we* are not going to do anything of the sort! I have a cousin who's in the construction business, and he knows how to handle dynamite. If you have found any bone holes, he and I will come back to Weatherend, and we will dig the bones out of the holes, plant some dynamite, and blast those accursed statues into powder. There will be considerable risk, and I don't want you and Myra anywhere in the vicinity when the real dirty work is being done."

Miss Eells was hopping mad. "Now look here, Emerson! I know I'm a bit on the clumsy side, but I'm as brave as you are and maybe braver! When we were kids, who was it who went out in Farmer Swenson's field and dared the bull to come after her? You were hiding somewhere under Dad's car! And who was it who went down in the cellar of our house at night to see if there really was a ghost there? Hmm, who? I can understand why you might want to keep Anthony out of this, but I'll be darned if I can see why *I* should stay home and twiddle my thumbs!"

Emerson was aghast. He was the head of his own law firm, and he was used to giving orders and making people toe the line. But he had always been a little bit scared of his sister. Beads of sweat broke out on his forehead, and he took out his handkerchief and dabbed at his face. "Well, we could work out something, I'm sure," he muttered, throwing nervous sidelong looks at his sister.

Miss Eells grinned. "Do you mean, dear brother Em," she said in a mocking tone, "that I can actually be of *some* small use to you?"

Emerson took off his wristwatch and wound it busily. "Of course," he said in a low voice, without looking up. "We've always done things together. But perhaps maybe to start with we could, uh, well . . . carry out the first part of my plan the way I've outlined it?" Emerson paused and glanced questioningly at his sister. "Okay?"

"I'll think about it," said Miss Eells, and she bit her lip to keep from laughing.

And so it was arranged. The three of them would meet on Saturday, the first of December, to implement step one in Emerson's plan. Anthony also wanted to help the demolition squad later, but he didn't have the power to change Emerson's mind. To make Anthony feel better, Emerson told him how smart he was for making the copy of old Mr. Borkman's journal and added that it was likely to be useful in their fight against Anders Borkman's evil plans.

"After all," he said, "if Borkman stole the journal back from you—and it looks very much as if that is what happened—then it must be important to him. As far as I'm concerned, most of it is gibberish, and we've deciphered the important information already. But maybe if we study it carefully, it will yield some more meaning."

After some additional planning Anthony, Miss Eells, and Emerson went back to the parlor and played

Scrabble for a while. Amid the good-natured post-game bickering between Miss Eells and her brother, Anthony noticed that it was way past ten o'clock. His mother always got upset when he stayed out late, and he did not want her to start calling around to locate him. So he said his good-byes hurriedly and left.

As Anthony disappeared down the walk the other two stood in the doorway and watched him go. Miss Eells looked worried.

"Do you think it was wise to include Anthony in this thing?" she said, turning to Emerson. "What if something goes wrong?"

Emerson smiled and blew a stream of pipe smoke into the chilly night air. "I haven't miscalculated," he said coolly. "We're not going to be at the estate very long, and it'll be during the day, when the power of those evil stones is at its weakest. We'll be in and out of there before Borkman knows what hit him."

CHAPTER SEVEN

Saturday the first of December was a cold, windy day. Anthony woke up feeling anxious, like a soldier who has just been told that he is going to be parachuting into enemy territory. For days he had been brooding about Anders Borkman and the evil ring of stones. Sometimes the whole situation seemed completely unbelievable. Could that nasty, cold-blooded man really control the weather? A year ago Anthony would have said that the idea was just too fantastic. But he had seen a lot of strange things lately, and Emerson had made him realize that Borkman's statues were as dangerous—in their way —as atomic bombs. But even though Anthony was pretty scared, in the midst of his fear he knew an expert was on his side. Emerson Eells had studied magic, and he would use his knowledge to take care of Mr. Borkman and his crazy plans.

Anthony whiled away the morning. He rode down to the A&P with his dad and helped him bring the groceries home. Then he went out to the garage and watched his brother, Keith, tinker with a car. But while Keith tried to explain to Anthony about pistons and cylinder heads and camshafts Anthony's mind was elsewhere. He was thinking about three o'clock that afternoon and the four grim stone statues.

At a little after two Anthony went into the house and told his mother that he was going over to the high school athletic field to play touch football with some friends. Then he put on his red leather cap and his winter coat and headed off to begin his secret mission.

Number 611 Pine Street, the home of Miss Eells, was the first stop. When he got there, he saw a gray truck parked in the driveway next to the house; it had a blue gas flame in a yellow halo and the words HOOSAC GAS CO. painted on the side. Next to the truck stood Emerson Eells, wearing gray coveralls and a peaked cap with the gas company emblem on the front. He was smoking a cigarette and trying to look nonchalant. Anthony thought Miss Eells was right: Emerson did not look like a gas man. He seemed too . . . well, too intellectual. Perhaps Borkman would think that Emerson was an out-of-work professor who had to take a job with the gas company to make a living.

The front door of the house opened, and Miss Eells

stepped out, looking like she was ready to go for a hike in the woods. She wore a heavy brown tweed sweater, padded blue winter jacket, sensible brown oxfords, and white sweat socks. Anthony wondered what was in the big green bulging patent leather purse she was carrying.

Emerson spotted the purse too and immediately grew alarmed. "What the dickens have you got there? Are you taking penny rolls to the bank?"

"It's Grampa's old Colt forty-four dragoon pistol," she said, pulling it halfway out of her purse. "It doesn't have any bullets, but it looks impressive."

Emerson made a great effort to control himself. "My dear sister," he said in a tight, strained voice, "we are not going to the Battle of Antietam. We are taking part in a quick, smooth undercover operation. Please dump that piece of antique artillery in the house and come along! We're behind schedule—I told Borkman that I was coming to read his meter at three."

Miss Eells glanced disconsolately at the handbag. Then she disappeared into the house. When she came back, she was carrying a battered old field hockey stick.

"Can I take this? It'll make me feel better if I've got *something* to defend myself with."

Emerson covered his face with his hand. "Oh, all *right*! Jump in the back of the truck and let's get *moving*!"

Out into the country they drove, past the Rolling Stone library and down into a hollow overhung by bare, wintry trees. After about ten minutes they saw a high stone wall topped with spikes. In a few places the old wall had collapsed, but it had been repaired and reinforced by a shiny, new chain-link fence topped by three strands of barbed wire. Finally the truck rounded a curve, and Anthony saw the main entrance of the estate with its grim-looking gatehouse, boarded windows, and two stone gateposts. The gate was new, made of tubular steel and chain links, and a heavy steel lock held its two sections together.

"Looks friendly, doesn't it?" said Emerson as he stopped the truck in front of the gate.

Anthony and Miss Eells were crouching behind the front seat so they couldn't be seen from outside.

"What's going on, Em?" whispered Miss Eells hoarsely. "Are there guards or machine-gun nests? I can't see a blasted thing down here!"

"There aren't any guards," said Emerson calmly. "The whole place is remote-controlled. There's a squawk box on one of the gateposts that you can yell into, and if Borkman wants you in, he just pushes a button and the gates swing open. Simple, eh? Now you just wait here while I go talk to our friend."

Miss Eells spoke again, and she sounded worried. "Em? I have a bad feeling about all this. I think we ought to turn around and skedaddle back home while we have the chance."

Emerson snorted. "Oh, piffle, Myra! There are no guards on the estate—I think Borkman is too cheap to hire any—and I've asked that that stupid dog be chained up while I'm there. Put all your worries out of your mind! Remember I wouldn't have led you two up here if I thought there was any real chance you'd get hurt. So stop fussing!"

Emerson got out of the truck, walked toward the gates, and spoke into the box. Sure enough, there was a loud *bzzzz-click!*, and then the gates swung open. With a jaunty, cocksure smile on his face Emerson got back into the truck and slammed the door.

"See?" he said as he started the engine. "No problems."

Miss Eells made no reply, but in the darkness she reached out and squeezed Anthony's hand.

"Good luck, kid," she whispered.

They heard the gates swing behind them with a loud crash as they drove on. Then Emerson put on the brakes again.

"Okay, everybody!" he said brusquely. "Out you go! The tennis court is off to the left, and the grove with the statues is beyond it. Just do what I've asked—nothing else. I'll come back pretty soon and give a little beep on the horn. Be there when I honk."

Anthony and Miss Eells clambered out of the back of the truck, pushed the doors shut, and the truck sped away in a cloud of exhaust smoke. Anthony stood blinking in the bright sunlight. Then he turned and looked at Miss Eells, and he almost laughed. She was holding the hockey stick upright like a shepherd's crook. It made her look like an elderly lady impersonating Bo-Peep or the world's oldest field hockey goalie.

"Laugh now," said Miss Eells, brandishing the stick. "We may need this dumb thing before today is over with." She straightened her glasses on her nose and marched off across the matted, frosty grass with Anthony following behind her.

They paused to look at the ruined tennis court. The concrete playing surface was cracked and pitted, and the wire fence that surrounded it was rusted and full of holes. The little building at one end had once had a red tile roof, but now half the tiles lay in broken, crumbling heaps on the ground.

Miss Eells sighed and looked around. "This place is certainly a mess, isn't it? Did I ever tell you that I was Singles Tennis Champion of my class at Bryn Mawr in 1906? Well, I was. But time's a-wasting! We'd better go have a look at those ghastly statues."

Anthony and Miss Eells tramped on, past the tennis court and over a patch of weedy ground. Dead thistles hovered on tall stalks all around them, and the yellow grass felt spongy under their feet. Straight ahead was the cedar grove. It looked forbidding, a mass of inky green shadows under the pale, wintry sun. When they got to the grove, Miss Eells and Anthony found that there was no path leading to the open space in the middle, so they had to shove their way through the dark, perfumy boughs, which kept slapping them in the face and scratching at their arms and legs. As they battled their way through, the boughs resisted, as if they possessed their own hostile will. Anthony felt fear rising inside him, but he fought the panic down and struggled on. By the time he had reached the inner circle he was weak and gasping for breath.

There before them were the four dark, rugged stones, looking every bit as sinister as they had in the garage. The eerie, staring faces and clawlike, groping hands gave the odd feeling that they were . . . well, somehow *alive*. It would not have surprised Anthony if those four masses of stone suddenly turned into pillars of smoke and spewed forth monstrous, fearful shapes. Anthony was glad he was not going to be here when Emerson and Miss Eells came at night to destroy them.

Anthony looked at Miss Eells, and she glanced quickly back at him. Her face was red, and her hair was mussed, but she was trying hard not to act nervous or frightened.

"Well, now," said Miss Eells, forcing her mouth into a businesslike frown. "We'd better get moving, because we don't have a lot of time. Let's find those holes, then hotfoot it back to the tennis court and wait for Emerson to show up." And with that she put down the hockey stick, stepped forward, and started to examine one of the stones. Cautiously she put out her hand to touch the rough granite surface.

"Ow!" she yelled, jerking her hand back. Her hand flew to her mouth, and she sucked at her fingertips. "Ow, ow, ow! That is *hot*, Anthony. Be careful!"

Anthony was startled. How could the stones be that hot? The sun hung low in the sky, and it was a cold December afternoon. Then Anthony realized that he was sweating. The air inside this circle of trees was stuffy and humid.

"Lucky I brought some gloves," said Miss Eells in a tight, strained voice. She unzipped a side pocket of her jacket and pulled out two dirt-caked gardening gloves. She put them on and grimly stepped forward again. Anthony hadn't brought any gloves—he'd have to do his investigating without touching the stones.

Slowly Anthony's eyes traveled up and down the surface of one of the stone pillars. A gaping skull mask glared down at him, and he flinched as his eyes met this cold, inhuman stare. He shuffled to one side and went on examining the stone. Ah! There it was! A round spot about the size of a penny. Clever old Emerson Eells was right again!

"I found one, Miss Eells!" Anthony called, pointing triumphantly.

Miss Eells smiled and nodded. "Great! Mark the place with chalk and keep hunting. I haven't found any yet, but they may be cleverly— Hah! There's mine! Okay, we're really doing great!" Excitedly she fumbled in another pocket and came up with a squarish lump of white chalk. She marked the plugged hole with a small X and moved on to the next stone.

It took Anthony and Miss Eells only about twenty minutes to locate all four holes. But by the time they were finished they felt as if they had been in this evil, airless place for hours. Anthony found that he was beginning to imagine things . . . at least he hoped that he was imagining them. He kept thinking that the carvings on the stones were *moving*. When he looked one way, he would see—out of the corner of his eye—something shifting, just a bit, on one of the other pillars. And more than ever now he found that he was having trouble breathing. It was getting harder and harder to fight down the panic. He wanted to leave; he wanted to leave now.

"Come on, Miss Eells!" said Anthony, grabbing his friend by the arm. "We've marked all the holes, so let's just . . ." Anthony's voice trailed away. He saw, to his horror, that Miss Eells was just standing there with a glazed look on her face and her arms hanging limp at her sides.

Anthony hesitated a moment. Then he seized her by the shoulder and shook her violently. "Hey, Miss Eells! What's the matter? Are you okay? Please say something!"

"Wha . . . wha . . ." muttered Miss Eells thickly. "Who are . . . uh, I mean . . ." And with that she came to with a jolt. She looked about wildly—at the four grim dark stones, at the circle of shadowy trees, and at Anthony.

"What . . . what was I doing?" she asked in a wondering, scared voice. "No, don't tell me—I don't want to know. You're right. We've got to get out. Are you ready?"

Anthony nodded. He picked up the hockey stick and handed it to Miss Eells. Then the two of them plunged back into the cedar boughs. It was even harder going out than coming in, but somehow they made it. They reeled into the open, and after several nervous backward glances they headed toward the tennis court. When they got there, they did not stop but continued on till they got to the road. Emerson had told them that they were supposed to hide in the ruined building, but they'd had enough of enclosed spaces for now. They felt safer, somehow, just along the shoulder of the road.

They waited. Fifteen minutes passed, then thirty, forty-five, and then a full hour. The shadows of the roadside trees grew longer and longer. Then the sun set behind the distant hills, and the sky grew darker. With a sick, tight feeling in his stomach Anthony knew that something had gone wrong.

He peered anxiously up the winding drive. The white gravel of the road glimmered vaguely in the gathering darkness. When he spoke, his voice was a trembling whisper.

"Miss Eells? Where . . . where's Emerson? What's wrong? How come he hasn't come back?"

Miss Eells's face was pale and drawn. She bit her lip and shook her head despondently. "I don't know, Tony . . . I just don't know." She paced up and down a bit, and then lost her temper. She picked up a stone and threw it at the tennis-court fence. "Blast my brother!" she exclaimed in an angry, tearful voice. "He *always* knows what to do! You can't tell him anything, you can't warn him or make him cautious when there's every reason to be cautious. Em's got it all figured out! Oh, this is awful, Anthony! What on earth are we going to do?"

Anthony looked around. He felt completely helpless. It was so dark that the tennis-court building was just a shadow, and he couldn't see the evil grove of trees at all. Once again panic was creeping over him. He wanted to get out of this awful, unnerving place, even though he knew that he ought to stay and try to help Emerson. He wanted to be brave, but he was terribly, terribly afraid.

Once again he seized Miss Eells's arm and squeezed it. "We've got to go!" he hissed. "They'll get us if we don't!"

Miss Eells pulled herself together. She set her jaw grimly and got a firm grip on her hockey stick. "I want to go running up the road to Borkman's house, burst in on him, and pound knobs on his rotten skull, but I suspect that would not be a very bright idea," she said in a low voice. "No, you're right—we've got to escape. But how? You saw the walls and the cyclone fence—this place is like a prison. And we didn't bring a flashlight with us. We're going to go stumbling about like a couple of blind bats in a brewery."

Miss Eells paused. She pounded the butt of her hockey stick on the ground, took a deep breath, and let it out. She had made up her mind.

"Okay, Tony," she said in a determined voice. "We

may be doomed, but at least we'll go down fighting. We have to go back down the road toward the gate and then pick our way along the fence till we find a weak spot. I saw a couple of places where the wall was broken and had been patched with chain-link fence. Maybe we can climb the wrecked wall and get over the fence somehow."

Miss Eells and Anthony started walking. The road was a pale ribbon in the starlight, and all around them the shadows of trees and bushes seemed to close in and hover over them. The silence was unnerving. Anthony would have been glad to hear the sound of a car passing on the road beyond the wall, or wind in the trees, or even the hooting of an owl. But there was nothing, nothing but the sound of their footfalls on the gravel.

Finally Anthony saw the dim outline of the main gate.

"Hey, Miss Eells!" he yelled, waving his arm. "Look!"

"Great!" she muttered. "Now all we have to do is find a weak spot in the wall. Maybe over there—"

Miss Eells never finished her sentence. She heard a noise, an odd rustling. Fearfully she peered off to her left and saw, by the side of the road, a heap of dead leaves. And though no wind was blowing, the leaves were stirring uneasily. As Anthony and Miss Eells watched, the leaves began to whirl and spin.

"Run, Anthony!" yelled Miss Eells suddenly. And with that they were off, racing across the grass. The rustling behind them rose to an angry whirring. Miss

Eells and Anthony ran faster, blindly, into the dark. Now they saw looming before them the great black shadow of the wall that surrounded the estate, and turning sharply to the right, they began to run alongside it. More dead leaves began to stir. As he went pounding along, full speed, Anthony saw a leaf rise up and fly at his face. It brushed his cheek, and he gave a wild yell. The leaf had cut his cheek. He felt the sticky wetness of blood. Miss Eells cried out, and he knew she must have been cut too.

"Up there, up there!" she yelled, waving her hockey stick as she swerved off suddenly into the shadow of the wall. "Wall's . . . broken . . ." She gasped. "Climb it quick. These leaves'll . . . kill us!"

Without knowing what he was doing or why, Anthony ran off after Miss Eells. In seconds he was totally swallowed up by the darkness. Stumbling against a heap of stones, he fell forward onto his hands and knees. But Miss Eells had already dropped the hockey stick and was scrambling madly up a broken rocky slope. Anthony pulled himself to his feet and hurled himself up the wall after her. There was the chain-link fence that had been used to patch this part of the wall. And above him, outlined against the starry sky, was Miss Eells. She was peeling off her padded jacket and yelling commands at Anthony. Despite his confusion and fear, he managed to make out what she was saying. He was supposed to throw his coat over the barbed wire at the top of the fence to protect himself when he jumped over it.

But as Anthony began unbuttoning his coat, a sound like a thousand angry bees rose from the darkness below them. A cloud of leaves had turned into a spiraling tornado that surrounded the two of them. Anthony covered his face with his hands and fell to his knees, screaming. There was no escape—he was going to die.

CHAPTER EIGHT

Every muscle in Anthony's body grew tense. He pressed his hands very hard against his face, digging the nails into his skin. Holding his breath, he waited for the horrible pain to begin. In his fevered brain a thought formed: *Please, let me just black out.* Any minute now, any second now, it would start, and then . . .

An icy mist blew over Anthony's body. That, and nothing more. For several seconds longer he held his rigid pose. Then he took his hands away from his face and looked around. Miss Eells was lying flat on the top of the wall, her hands over her head. She too straightened up and peered blearily around. The leaves were quiet; the whirring sound had stopped. Except for a couple of minor cuts and scrapes they were all right.

"Well, now!" said Miss Eells as she brushed dirt off her knees. "Life is full of surprises, isn't it? I thought we were going to be turned into hamburger. I guess Old Nasty up there in the mansion is toying with us, having his own ghoulish kind of fun. Let's clear out before our kindly host changes his mind. We'll have to leave our coats behind, but that's better than having our pelts nailed to Mr. Borkman's barn door, don't you think?"

Anthony nodded glumly. He took off his coat and draped it over the barbed wire. Then, gripping the top of the fence, he vaulted over and dropped to the ground. When he looked up he saw Miss Eells hanging by her hands from the top of the wall. She was afraid to let go.

"It's okay, Miss Eells!" Anthony called. "There's a big pile of leaves down here, and they'll—" Anthony clapped his hand to his mouth. He realized what he had just said.

"Break my fall?" said Miss Eells sarcastically. "Okay, one-two-three . . . *bombs away!*"

And she dropped into the leaf pile. She landed on her heels, wobbled a bit, and then fell over onto her back. Immediately she scrambled to her feet and glanced nervously around, as if she expected the leaves to leap up and attack her. But they lay quiet.

"Are you okay?" Anthony asked anxiously as he came running up to her.

"More or less," she said, sighing. "We'd better start hiking. It's at least nine miles back to Hoosac—maybe more. I'm glad I wore my sensible shoes."

"What about Emerson?" Anthony asked.

"There's not a blessed thing we can do about him," said Miss Eells, shaking her head gloomily.

Anthony and Miss Eells started walking. It was dark on the road at first, but later the moon rose over the trees and made the going a little easier.

Finally they arrived at the Rolling Stone library. And who should be sitting on the steps that led up the grassy bank but Emerson Eells.

"Em!" Miss Eells whooped joyfully, running toward him. "Em! It's you!" She threw her arms around her brother and gave him a big hug.

"Good evening," said Emerson, and he smiled in a dreamy, distant way. "Well, we didn't quite do what we set out to, did we?"

Miss Eells stared curiously at Emerson. Why was he acting so unbelievably calm? Then she hugged her brother again, hard. "I'm just glad you're okay!" She paused and again peered questioningly at him. "You are okay, aren't you?"

Emerson nodded. "I think so. I feel a bit dazed, but otherwise I'm all right. In case you're wondering, I've been teleported here. I got out of the truck and was starting up the walk when Borkman opened the door to the mansion and said, 'Enjoy your trip, Mr. Eells!' Then he raised his hand and *zippo!*—here I was, sitting on these blasted steps." He sighed and looked vaguely annoyed. "I'm afraid that I've underestimated Anders Borkman."

"What happened to the truck?" asked Anthony. His feet were sore from walking, and he would have liked to ride the rest of the way home.

Emerson shrugged. "It seems to have vanished. I've been waiting here for hours, hoping you would show up."

Miss Eells told Emerson they had found the holes in the four stone slabs. Strangely enough, he did not seem terribly pleased by this.

"Much good that information will do us," he snapped, shrugging. "If we go anywhere near the estate, Borkman will just teleport us back home. He's too strong for us— much too strong."

Miss Eells shook her head in despair. "What are we going to do? Just sit around while that monster cooks up a scheme that will destroy the world?"

Emerson gazed blandly at his sister. "Heavens, Myra, I don't think he means to do that! Now that I've seen him, I am convinced that he merely wants to be left alone with his barometers and weather magic. Oh, he may cause a thunderstorm or hailstorm from time to time, but I believe that's all he'll do. And who knows? Maybe he'll even find out something that will allow us to control the weather. What a wonderful boon that would be! I think we should leave Borkman alone. The only real danger would arise from our interfering with him."

Miss Eells and Anthony were stunned. They couldn't believe what Emerson was saying. He had led the expedition because he was convinced that Borkman's weather magic was a threat to the entire world. And now he seemed to think that Borkman was just a harmless crank. It was all very mysterious.

Miss Eells folded her arms and looked very hard at her brother for a long time. "Emerson," she said finally, "do you mean that you're going to just *give up*? That's not like you, not like you at all! Where did you get the idea that Borkman is merely fooling around with magic? You didn't think that before. What has come over you?"

Emerson avoided his sister's gaze. He looked off into space, and in the moonlight his expression seemed strangely peaceful, but also a bit stubborn. "Nothing has come over me," he said calmly. "I've . . . merely changed my mind, that's all." He got up and brushed dirt off the seat of his coveralls. "And now," he said in a cold and businesslike tone, "I think we had better head back to Hoosac. Myra, do you still have a key to this library? If so, I think we should call a taxi. Standing around in the night air is not going to do any of us a great deal of good."

Miss Eells and Anthony stared at each other, mystified. With a deep sigh Miss Eells reached into the pocket of her dress and pulled out a key ring.

When they were inside the library, Miss Eells called the Gegenfurtner Taxi Company, which was run by Ray Gegenfurtner, the son of an old friend of hers. She was sure that young Ray would drive them home without asking too many questions.

As they sat waiting for the cab to arrive, Anthony began thinking about what would happen to him when he got home. It was after eight, and it had been dark for a good three hours. Convincing his parents that he had been playing touch football all this time would be impossible. And what explanation could he give for losing his good winter coat? Anthony braced himself for the wrath that was to come.

When Anthony got home, he discovered that his worst fears had come true. His mother was furious. It seemed that she had been calling everyone to find out where he was, including nosy Mrs. Schweikert, who had told her she had seen Anthony heading up Pine Street toward Miss Eells's house earlier that day. If there was anything that Mrs. Monday hated, it was lying. And so she told Anthony that while he could go to school and work at the library in the afternoons, otherwise he had to stay at home for two whole weeks.

". . . and I hope you'll realize that I'm doing this to teach you a lesson," she said. "I don't like making up stories and sneaking around. Most of all I don't like your hanging around with somebody who's such a bad influence. Everybody in this town is talking about that old Miss Eells and how crazy she is. Why do you want to pal around with a screwball like that? Aren't you ashamed of yourself?"

"Yes, Mom," said Anthony. But actually he wasn't ashamed at all. He went upstairs to his room and bolted the door. Then he sat down on his bed and cried. How could his mother be so unfair? How could she have misjudged Miss Eells so terribly? Miss Eells was a wonderful person who was in a lot of trouble, and all Mrs. Monday could say was that she was a nut. In the midst of his anger and tears Anthony wondered what his mom would have said if he had told her about the trip out to the Borkman estate. *Yes, Mom, we're trying to save the world from a crazy guy who's using magic statues to cause terrible weather.* Anthony smiled through his tears as he imagined his mother chuckling at this. She would think he was just joking around. The trouble was, the stuff about Borkman was true. Anthony relapsed into gloom again. *What were they going to do?* They had tried Emerson's plan, and it had failed. He and Miss Eells had found the holes in the statues, but now Emerson insisted that there was no need to destroy them, that Borkman was not evil, as they had thought. Emerson's change of heart was very confusing. It had left Anthony worried and disheartened. Could there be something wrong with him? Had he been hypnotized by Borkman? Or was Emerson simply smarter than Anthony? Did he know things that Anthony and Miss Eells didn't?

Anthony's brain was whirling—nothing made sense anymore. With a shuddering sob he pulled himself together. He blew his nose loudly and started undressing. He wanted to take a shower and then go sit in his pajamas in front of the TV set with his father and brother until it was time to go to bed.

But suddenly Anthony heard something: a rattling sound like rain against the windowpane, only louder. He rushed to the window and looked down into the yard. Under the apple tree, bathed in the light of a cold, frosty moon, stood a small shadowy figure. Terror clutched at Anthony's heart. Who—or what—was down there, waiting for him? Anthony forced himself to look again. And then he almost laughed—it was Miss Eells! Quickly he raised the window and stuck his head out.

"Anthony!" Miss Eells called hoarsely. "Come on down! I need to talk to you! It's important!"

CHAPTER NINE

Anthony wanted to rush downstairs right away and find out what was on Miss Eells's mind. But he hesitated. He was supposed to be confined to quarters, and if his mother caught him sneaking out, she would blow her top like Old Faithful.

"Anthony, please come down!" Miss Eells called again. There was a pleading, desperate sound in her voice. How could he refuse her?

"Just a minute, Miss Eells!" he called. He padded over to the door, opened it, and listened. From downstairs came the sound of the television. His parents and Keith were still watching. Quickly Anthony took off his slippers and bathrobe and got dressed. Then he opened his desk drawer, took out a key, stepped into the hall, and locked his door. Mrs. Monday was nosy, but when Anthony locked his door, she usually respected his privacy. With the key in his pocket he tiptoed toward the playroom, where he and Keith had goofed around together when they were small. At the far end of the room was a door that led to the attic, and next to it was a tall sash window that looked out over the roof of the back porch. Anthony walked to the window, unfastened the catch, and slid it open. He eased himself onto the shingles and then carefully picked his way down to the edge of the roof. A ladder leading down to the ground was bolted to one of the porch columns for use as a fire escape. Quickly Anthony clambered down, hurried around the corner of the house, and almost ran into Miss Eells, who was pacing nervously under the apple tree.

"Anthony!" she exclaimed in a loud stage whisper. "I'm sorry I had to contact you in such a dramatic fashion, but I'm afraid to use the phone." Miss Eells paused and glanced furtively around. Then she went on, in a hurried, anxious voice. "Look, I'm worried sick. Something's the matter with Emerson. He left a couple of hours ago. Just left, without saying good-bye! I'm really concerned about the way he's been acting lately. You know how fussy he is about his belongings? Well, when he took off today, he left his best camel's-hair overcoat in the front hall closet and all four of the meerschaum pipes! Can you *imagine*? He takes them with him *everywhere*!"

"Maybe he was in a hurry," said Anthony. This was

not a very helpful comment, but it was the only one he could think of.

"Hurry, shmurry!" said Miss Eells, waving her hand impatiently. "He's *never* in too much of a hurry to take his pipes! We know that Borkman used his magic to hypnotize me into making a scene in the library. And we're also fairly certain that he did the same thing to you so you would give the diary to him. Well, he's done something like that to Emerson."

Miss Eells paused. Tears came to her eyes, and she shook her head in a grief-stricken way. "Oh, my poor brother! We've got to do something!" She set her jaw and looked very determined. Then she laid her hand on Anthony's arm and stared at him, hard. "And we've got to do it soon!" she added in a low, urgent voice. "You and I will have to go it alone."

Anthony swallowed hard. "Alone?"

Miss Eells nodded solemnly. "Who else is there? Emerson is out of the fight, for now. And we can't very well go down to the police station and say, 'Excuse me, Officer Swett, but there's a man on an estate near here who's planning to use black magic and lousy weather to wipe out the population of the world.' I mean, I'm already suspected of being a dangerous lunatic, and talk like that would only confirm everybody's suspicions. So we have to try to do what we can ourselves. We can't try to blow up the statues, because it would be too dangerous. But there are other things we can do. I want you to meet me over at my house tomorrow night, so we can—"

"I can't meet you," said Anthony, cutting her off. "I have to stay in nights because I lied to Mom and ran off with you guys."

Miss Eells stared at Anthony in disbelief. "Oh, great! Wait, I know! I'll meet you down at the library. You can go to work, can't you?"

Anthony nodded.

"I know I've been suspended, but I can still walk in and out of the stupid place if I want to. We need to have a place to confer, because we have to go over your copy of old Borkman's journal to see if there's anything in it that can help us. I've been rereading it, and that old buzzard may have had second thoughts about the horrors that he intended to unleash. He says in one place that 'he who can read the riddles contained herein will turn back the storm-tossed waves.' And there are other hints. I know that Emerson thought the journal was mostly nonsense, but I'm not so sure."

Miss Eells paused and scratched her chin thoughtfully. "Maybe we can use one of the empty offices. Elvira Pratt owes me a favor. All right. Monday afternoon at the library! In the meantime I'll try to work on the journal at home. Well, you'd better get back to your room before your mom finds out you're missing. God knows what would happen if she found you out here with me!"

Anthony hurriedly said good-bye and started climbing the ladder. *Don't worry, Miss Eells*, he said under his breath. *We'll win!* He had a sudden terrifying vision of a world devastated by windstorms and lightning. Of caved-in houses, roofless barns, and trees mowed down by violent gales. Of floods, and forests set on fire by lightning bolts. How was he, a fourteen-year-old kid, and Miss Eells, an eccentric little old lady who stuck her foot into wastebaskets and knocked plates off tables, going to stop this from happening? Anthony felt hopelessness and despair rising inside him. But he fought them down and climbed on.

On Monday after school Anthony hurried to the library as fast as he could. Miss Pratt was sitting at the front desk, and the expression on her face would have curdled milk.

"She's up in the Winterborn Reading Room," she said through her teeth. "I told her to hang a Room Not in Use sign outside so you two could be alone and do . . . whatever it is you're supposed to be doing. And you'd better not tell anybody I let you use that room."

Anthony hurried away, walking swiftly along the slippery tile floor. He stopped in front of the Winterborn Reading Room and, after glancing quickly at the sign on the knob, rapped sharply, twice. There was a pause; then the door opened just a crack, and Miss Eells peered out. When she saw it was Anthony, she flung the door wide.

"Hi, partner!" she said, grinning. "Come on in."

Anthony entered, and Miss Eells locked the door. The Winterborn Reading Room was small and comfortable, with a fireplace, lots of overstuffed chairs in flowered upholstery, lamps, and footstools. Not far from the fireplace was a long, old-fashioned library table. It usually stood against the wall, but Miss Eells had dragged it out to the middle of the room so that she and Anthony could use it to look at the copy of Borkman's journal. Piled nearby were books: *A History of Hoosac County*, *Peculiarities of American Cities*, and *Eminent Minnesotans*. There was a pot of hot coffee on a warmer and Coke in an ice bucket.

For hours Anthony and Miss Eells pored through the books and papers. They scribbled notes and conferred about the meaning of some obscure passage in the journal. Miss Eells spilled coffee on the floor, and once when she tried to stick a pencil in the bun on top of her head, she stabbed herself in the forehead. And, as she often did when she was working hard, she mumbled to herself. She said things like "*Sonorous bus* . . . now what on earth can that mean?" and "*Pam* . . . could be some friend of his, but I always heard the old coot didn't have any friends." Anthony leafed through the books and kept wishing he was smarter than he was. He tried to force his brain to work harder, but all he got for his troubles was a headache. Then suddenly it occurred to him that he was overlooking something pretty obvious: there were words and phrases in the journal that kept repeating. Sometimes the word or phrase would be scrawled across a whole page. Sometimes it would be on a page with other notes but carefully underlined. Were these the riddles that had to be solved, if the evil plan was to be thwarted? Anthony made a list of the repeated words and phrases:

> PAM
> PAM UNDER THE CRACK OF NOON
> THE SIGN OF THE INVERTED TORCH
> *Does the sonorous bus go ____-____?*
> FOR THE BLOOD IS THE LIFE
> *There are openings in the choir*
> *of the Blessed Virgin.*

Anthony looked at the list and sighed. It really was not terribly helpful. *PAM* was obviously somebody named Pamela, but as for the rest . . . well, it was utter gibberish as far as he was concerned. He showed it to Miss Eells, and she mumbled some of the phrases aloud. Anthony went to the ice bucket and opened a bottle of Coke. As he swigged, Miss Eells kept looking at the list, leafing through books, and jotting things down on a long yellow legal pad. Anthony glanced at the clock on the mantel. It was almost six, and he was feeling very hungry. But just as he was about to say something Miss Eells let out a bloodcurdling screech.

"*This is it! This is it!*" she yelled, waving the battered old volume entitled *Eminent Minnesotans.* "It was right here all the time—I was just too lazy to read all the stupid fine print! Look!"

When she had calmed down a bit, Miss Eells laid the book on the table. She explained quickly to Anthony that it had biographical articles on famous people who had lived in Minnesota and included one on J. K. Borkman. She had read it through once, without finding anything interesting. But the second time she noticed a footnote number in the last paragraph about Borkman's death. Now she flipped to the back and gave the book to Anthony to read:

[5] Mr. J. K. Borkman made elaborate preparations for his burial while he was still alive. He designed his own mausoleum and gave the builders careful instructions about the decorations that were to be placed on the doors and walls of the tomb. Every detail of the building was personally approved by him. He even designed an elaborate device for sealing the tomb chamber, and the secret of this device was known only to him and the undertakers. The Borkman mausoleum stands in St. Boniface's Cemetery in Duluth, not far from St. Scholastica's College. It is large and impressive and is done in a combination of the Classical and Egyptian Revival styles. Columns with lotus-shaped capitals flank the massive bronze doors, and sculpted on the doors, in high relief, are two inverted torches. These are, as is well known, symbols of mortality. . . .

Anthony looked up. Miss Eells was right—this *was* important! *The sign of the inverted torch* was one of the clues he had picked out. And then, suddenly, another idea hit him, and he laughed.

Miss Eells stared at him. "All right, I give up! What's so funny?"

"It's just that dumb old joke!" said Anthony. "Old Mr. Borkman is buried up in Duluth, and there's this joke that goes 'Does this bus go to Duluth?', and the answer is 'No, this bus goes beep-beep!' "

At first Miss Eells didn't get it. She wrinkled up her forehead and stared off into space. "Does this bus . . ." she muttered, and then she paused and chewed her lip. Suddenly her face lit up. "Hah! To Du-*luth*! Toodle-*oot*! Not beep-beep! And that's one of our clues, isn't it? The sonorous bus! If there's some way of stopping young Borkman from carrying out his father's plans, it seems we'll find it in that cemetery in Duluth. Well, that settles it! We have to go there."

Anthony's head was still spinning. Miss Eells was going too fast for him. "But what about *Pam* and *the crack of noon* and the rest of the clues?"

Miss Eells shrugged. "I suspect they will become clearer when we arrive at the cemetery. Are you coming with me?"

Anthony felt awful. His mother would never allow him to go away with Miss Eells. But maybe he should just leave without permission. After all, Miss Eells needed him. Anders Borkman had to be stopped.

Miss Eells looked at him sympathetically. She knew what he was going through, but she also knew how important it was for him to join her. The idea of driving all the way to Duluth—over two hundred miles—by herself, was harrowing. Also, Anthony was good with tools, and he could break into Borkman's tomb. Without him, Miss Eells thought, the mission might end in total disaster.

She took hold of Anthony's arm and stared at him hard. "Young man," she said, "a lot may depend on what you decide to do. I don't want to sound melodramatic, but you know that Anders Borkman is trying to destroy the world. Now, I *could* go by myself. But I'm a lousy, nervous driver, and as for breaking into the tomb . . . well, I have trouble opening a can of beans. So, a lot depends on you. I know you think your Mom'll massacre you if you disobey her. But if you *don't* come along, there may not be any Mom or Dad to come home to. I'm going to be making some rather large sacrifices myself. My hearing before the Library Board is tomorrow at noon. If we leave for Duluth tomorrow morning, I won't be there." Miss Eells paused and relaxed her grip on Anthony's arm. "You will come with me, won't you?"

Anthony had never felt more miserable in his life. He licked his lips and tried to avoid Miss Eells's earnest gaze. His stomach was all knotted up, and he felt so incredibly tense that he wanted to run around the room screaming. The marble clock on the mantel ticked quietly. Finally Anthony allowed his eyes to meet hers. He knew he ought to help her . . . and yet he kept thinking about the long, lonely drive up to Duluth and the terror that surely awaited them. What if Anders Borkman was using magic to listen in on their conversations right now? If so, he'd find some way of stopping them. And the things he'd do to them would not be pleasant. So far he had just been fooling around with them because he was sure they couldn't really do anything to stop him. But if Borkman ever thought that Anthony and Miss Eells could actually wreck his plans . . .

Anthony closed his eyes and gritted his teeth. He was scared, but he just couldn't let his friend go alone. He opened his eyes, looked at Miss Eells, and forced his mouth up into a wan little smile.

"Okay," he said quietly. "I'll go with you. When do we leave?"

CHAPTER TEN

At five A.M. the next morning Anthony awoke with a
jolt. He hadn't dared set his alarm, but fortunately he
had that built-in wake-up system that some people have.
The room was pitch black, and as he dressed he felt as if
he were moving inside a strange dream. In his closet
was a battered leather satchel containing his tools: a
hammer, hacksaw, chisel, small crowbar, flashlight, and
a Boy Scout hatchet. He had also thrown in a couple of
Mounds bars and a sweat shirt. He thought about his
sleeping parents and brother and the dark menace that
hung over the town of Hoosac as he took the satchel
out. *"This isn't happening,"* Anthony muttered to himself.
He stumbled over into a corner of the room, found his
new red parka and his red leather cap, and put them on.

Well, he was as ready as he'd ever be. With one hand on the doorknob Anthony looked back into his dark room. The friendly illuminated face of his bedside clock hovered there, like a tiny moon. Suddenly he had an overwhelming desire to be five years old and sick in bed with the flu. He wanted to be tucked in and have meals brought up to him. He wanted to have his mother spoon syrups into his mouth and tell him that everything was going to be all right. Luckily the feeling passed, and he went out, closing the door softly behind him.

A few minutes later Anthony was standing on the front steps of the library, waiting for Miss Eells. It was a cold, raw morning, and a stiff wind was blowing. It made a hollow whistling sound through the trees of Levee Park. All around him Anthony could hear the bare branches creaking and groaning, although it was still too dark to see much. Suddenly he heard the sound of a car motor. A low, bulky shape was creeping up the circular drive in front of the library. Anthony could hardly bear to look. What if it was Anders Borkman? But to his great relief he heard the signal—three beeps of the car horn. It was Miss Eells after all.

Anthony picked up his satchel and raced toward the car. The passenger door was flung open, the dome light inside came on, and there was Miss Eells. She was quite a sight in baggy gym pants, a sweat shirt with *Hoosac A.C.* on the front, and tennis shoes. Her hair bun was slightly mussed and had two pencils stuck in it, and around her neck was a Saint Christopher medal on a chain. On the seat next to her was a folded road map and a brown paper bag that probably contained lunch.

"Hi, Anthony!" she said cheerfully. She seemed amazingly calm for someone who was going off on a dangerous mission.

Anthony threw his satchel into the backseat and climbed into the car. He was not terribly surprised by Miss Eells's outfit; after all, he had seen her in some pretty weird getups. But the medal puzzled him, and he asked about it.

"Oh, *that*!" said Miss Eells as she threw the car into gear and drove off. "Saint Christopher is the patron saint of travelers. This is going to be a pretty difficult trip, and I figured we might need some help from him before this adventure is over with."

The car started slowly down Levee Boulevard. Anthony was just settling himself back for the long drive when Miss Eells put on the brakes.

"Look!" she said, pointing excitedly.

Startled, Anthony sat up. It was still dark, but along the sidewalk he could see a row of streetlamps. Someone had just passed out of the circle cast by one lamp and into the gloom. Tensely Anthony waited for the figure to move into the light again. When it suddenly did, his jaw dropped. It was Mrs. Oxenstern! She was in a gym suit, and she was walking fast, heel-to-toe. Her stomach bobbled up and down as she went, and she pumped her fat arms vigorously.

Miss Eells covered her face with her hand. "I just don't

believe it! She must come out at this ungodly hour so no one will see her! Well, now I've seen everything." And with that, Miss Eells threw the car into gear again and roared off.

They drove down through the center of the sleeping city and across the great iron suspension bridge into Wisconsin. On they went, through small towns and across rolling acres of farm country. As they drove it got lighter outside but not much lighter; it was going to be a dark day. Miss Eells switched on the car radio. The weatherman reported that it would be cloudy, clearing toward evening. But it occurred to Miss Eells—and to Anthony—that there might be storms that couldn't be predicted. As they drove, Miss Eells's cheerfulness gave way to worry and tension. She told Anthony that she had tried to phone Emerson several times but had never gotten an answer. She also wondered if they might be going on a wild-goose chase. The "clues" in old Bork-man's diary might not be clues at all.

"Nevertheless," said Miss Eells with a sigh, "it's better to try than not to. All last night I dreamed about those four standing stones. Only they weren't in that circle of cedars. They were on a grassy hill, with a dark moun-tain in the background. It was like that vision I had when the blue fog from that book put me in that terrible trance in the library. Anders Borkman was there, standing inside the circle in a black robe. And every time he flung his hands in the air, lightning bolts came crashing down from the sky and thunder rumbled in the distance. You and

Emerson and I were watching, but we couldn't do anything. And then an ice storm started, and my face was covered with ice and I couldn't see or breathe. I woke up, gasping and choking. It was just awful. It may have been just a crazy dream, but still . . . well, it may have been a warning of things to come." She paused and then went on. "Do you know what really drives me crazy? I feel like I ought to know the answer to that clue about the choir of the Blessed Virgin. I mean, I'm a Catholic and all. But so far, it's as clear as mud."

On Miss Eells chatted as she drove while Anthony just listened and watched the scenery go by. Around ten A.M. they stopped at a restaurant in Eau Claire, and Anthony had a big breakfast. Miss Eells ate the sandwich and banana that she had brought, and then they drove on. The farmhouses got fewer and fewer, and the fields looked wilder and more forsaken. And then it started to snow. At first there were just a few little twirling flakes, but soon it was coming down thick and fast. The road became a sparkling white track, and Anthony began to notice that the car was wavering from side to side.

"I think we're starting to skid," he said, giving Miss Eells a worried glance.

Miss Eells shrugged. "Don't worry, friend. I had my snow . . ." Her voice trailed off. She made a choking noise, and then she swore and pounded her fist on the steering wheel. "Oh, *no*, I don't *believe* it. How could I have been such an idiotic *fool*?"

Anthony stared blankly. "What's wrong?"

"Oh, nothing much," said Miss Eells bitterly. "I just forgot to have my snow chains put on, that's all. Let's hope this snow doesn't get so bad that we'll have problems— Oh, God! Look!"

Up ahead of them a dog had wandered out onto the road. He was directly in front of the car, just staring stupidly around him. Miss Eells hit the brakes, and the car skidded. The dog ran off, and she took her foot off the brake, but it was too late. The car began to fishtail. It swung into wider and wider arcs. "Hang on!" she yelled, and Anthony clutched frantically at the door handle. Rear end first, the car rolled off the road and down a steep, bumpy, rocky incline. Something hard hit its underside with a loud *bongg!* and a sickening jolt. Anthony thought they were going to flip over. But the car just kept on rolling till it came to a jarring, tooth-rattling halt against the trunk of a tree.

Silence. Anthony sat dead still and listened to his pounding heart. Amazingly he wasn't injured. For what seemed like a long time, he stared straight ahead, up the steep rocky slope that was fast being covered by the swirling snow. Although he was afraid to look over and see how Miss Eells was doing, he finally forced himself. And there she sat, her hands folded in her lap and an utterly disgusted look on her face.

"Well, that was fun, wasn't it?" she said dryly. Then her voice broke, and it sounded as if she were going to cry. "Oh, Anthony!" she wailed. "What are we going to do? We can't push this car up that slope or drive it up.

We'll just have to sit here while the snow covers us up. It's all because I forgot to put on the stupid *snow chains*!"

"Don't worry," Anthony said. "We'll get there somehow. Everything'll be all right."

Miss Eells got out of the car and went around to the rear to inspect the damage. And Anthony, with a lot of slipping and sliding, managed to scale the steep bank and make it up to the road. He waved his arms frantically at about half a dozen cars, but they all just whizzed on past. At last a big red tow truck with a chain hoist came rolling past, and when Anthony motioned, it stopped. The white letters on the truck's door said JOHN JOHNSON TOWING   EAU CLAIRE, WIS.

Anthony ran up to the truck, and the driver rolled his window down. He was a middle-aged man with an oblong head, a long, blunt-ended nose, and a big sheaf of yellow hair that stuck out from under the baseball cap he was wearing.

"H'lo, young man. What's your problem? You lost?"

"No, no!" said Anthony, excitedly. He pointed off to the right, at the ditch. "Our car's down there! A dog ran in front of the car and Miss Eells and I ran off the road. Can you get us out?"

The man heaved a deep sigh and looked at his watch. "Oh, I spose so," he said wearily. "Anyway, I'll give it a try." He got out of the truck. Mumbling some more to himself, he loped over to the edge of the road and peered down. "We-ell . . ." he said slowly, "I think my cable'll just about reach that far. Like I said, we'll give 'er the old college try. Tell your friend to come on up here if she can. You guys can watch while I fix you up."

Anthony slipped back down the slope and helped Miss Eells make it to the road. The man turned on the amber flasher on top of his truck, and then he backed it up until the rear wheels were at the very edge of the ditch. From the derrick at the rear of the truck hung a woven steel cable with a big hook on the end. With the hook in his hand and the cable paying out slowly the man made his way down the slope toward the car. He hooked the cable under the front bumper of the Dodge, made sure the car's gears were in neutral, and then clambered back up to the truck and started the engine on the hoist. As he worked he sang a very monotonous song called "Yon Yonson" over and over in a strong Swedish accent:

> My name is Yon Yonson,
> Ay come from Vis-con-sin
> Ay work to de lumber hoosé de-ere
> When ay valk down de street
> Da people ay meet
> Dey say to me, "Vot is your na-ame?"
> And ay say,
> My name is Yon Yonson,
> Ay come from Vis-con-sin . . .

And on and on. After the man had sung the song through about ten times, Miss Eells and Anthony were pretty sick of it, but they were not about to complain. Mr. Johnson and his truck were—as far as they were concerned—sent from heaven. The hoisting engine whirred and slowly the poor, battered Dodge was hauled up out of the ditch. Miss Eells got her purse and some other important things out of the car. Then she and Anthony climbed into the cab with the driver and they drove back to Eau Claire.

A bit later Anthony and Miss Eells were sitting on a couple of rickety wooden chairs in a smelly, badly lit garage. The Dodge had just been lowered from the lift, and Mr. Johnson was standing before them, his long face even longer than usual.

"Broken axle?" asked Miss Eells, looking up. "Did you say broken *axle*?"

Mr. Johnson nodded glumly. "Yep. Musta hit a rock er somethin' on the way down. I can't fix it here—hafta send away to the Dodge people for a new one. My advice'd be, get a new car. Not worth fixin' in my opinion."

There was an uncomfortable pause. Miss Eells looked at Anthony and down at the floor. Then she turned to Mr. Johnson, and the expression on her face was one of utter hopelessness. She thought about the chances of her being able to pay for a new car. Very soon she would be unemployed: today was the day she was supposed to be appearing before the Library Board. But instead she was off on an improbable mission that had just turned into a super-impossible one. With difficulty Miss Eells pulled herself together. She heaved a deep sigh, put on her best businesslike attitude, and cleared her throat. "Hem! Well, Mr. Johnson, can we leave my poor vehicle here for a couple of days?"

Mr. Johnson looked hesitant. He scratched his long chin. "We-elll . . ." he said slowly, ". . . I got a lotta stuff out there in the back lot, but I guess one more hunka junk wouldn't matter none. Yeah, sure, you c'n leave it for a bit. But how're you gonna get to . . . didja say Duluth?"

"We really have to get there," said Anthony. "We . . . it's kind of an emergency."

"Yes," added Miss Eells, nodding. "It really is very important. I see by the sign over there that you rent cars. Could you possibly rent us one for a few days?"

Mr. Johnson's eyebrows rose, and he looked Miss Eells up and down. Miss Eells blushed, because she knew what he was thinking. Could an old lady who wore tennis shoes and gym pants and a Hoosac A.C. sweat shirt ever pay for a rented car? Silently Miss Eells cursed herself. Why had she decided to travel in this dumb outfit when she could have just carried the gym suit along to wear later? But then her pride welled up inside her. Who did Mr. Johnson think he was, anyway? She was a respectable citizen who had lived sixty-eight years without having been convicted of a major crime, and—until recently— had been regarded as a reasonable, solvent, hardworking person.

Slowly she stood up. She put on the most haughty expression she could manage, clutched her pocketbook to her breast, and said icily, "Mr. Johnson, my credit is perfectly good. You can call the First National Bank of

Hoosac if you want. I can write you a check for the towing job you did, and then—"

"Be s'prised if the banks was open," said Mr. Johnson, cutting her off. "Big storm down'n Hoosac—heard about it on the radio. Wind 'n' snow 'n' hail, t'beat the band! Funny kind of a storm—just started, all of a sudden, down there round Hoosac and La Crosse. Usually they come in from the north 'n' hit us first. We'll get it in an hour or so, I bet. That snow out there's just the beginning."

Mr. Johnson went back to rubbing his chin and thinking about whether or not Miss Eells was a good risk. Miss Eells and Anthony looked at each other. They were not worrying over credit ratings now. A cold fear was rising in their guts. Was this the start of the wild, world-ending storm that they had feared?

"Look here, Mr. Johnson," Miss Eells said angrily, "I haven't got time to sit here and grow moss on my north side while you make up your mind. It is very important that we get to Duluth as soon as possible, so if you don't mind, I'll settle our towing bill and then my young friend and I will go down the street and find a . . ."

Miss Eells's voice trailed off. She had taken one step toward the doorway of Mr. Johnson's office, but now she froze in her tracks. Anthony froze too, and stared. Somebody was standing in the entrance to the garage. It was a person that they knew very well but had not expected to see.

CHAPTER ELEVEN

There in the wide doorway stood Emerson Eells. In the stormy half-light he looked like a visitor from another world. He was wearing a black fur Alpine hat with a small red cockade on it and a gray winter coat with large black buttons. Oddly enough on his feet were pointed black leather shoes instead of boots or galoshes. And although the street outside looked slushy, Emerson's shoes were immaculately clean.

Miss Eells and Anthony looked quickly at each other, but neither of them moved an inch. Normally Miss Eells would have rushed over and thrown her arms around Emerson. But she was afraid. He had not been acting like himself when he left her house, and his sudden reappearance . . . Miss Eells bit her lip and tried to fight down the fear that was rising inside her. *How had Emerson known that she and Anthony would be here?*

"Hello, there!" he said, raising his mittened hand and waving. But the wave was a weak one, and his smile seemed cold and formal. His pale blue eyes glittered coldly behind his spectacles.

Again Miss Eells glanced nervously at Anthony. Then she took a couple of uncertain steps forward. "Em!" she exclaimed. "What . . . what on earth are you doing *here?* How did you know . . . I mean, I tried to get you on the phone, but . . ."

Emerson beamed reassuringly. "Oh, I just guessed," he said blandly. "I've always thought that I might be blessed with ESP or some such power. In any case I'm glad my instincts led me here." He glanced quickly toward Miss Eells's wrecked car. And he added, in the same calm, lilting tone, "I gather that you two are in need of some assistance. Am I right?"

Anthony watched Miss Eells intently, wondering what she would say. If Emerson was in the power of Anders Borkman, then would they want his help? Miss Eells walked slowly forward until she was standing only a few feet away from her brother. She stared steadily into his eyes.

"Em, are you all right?" she asked.

Emerson seemed slightly startled, but the bland smile did not fade. "Of course I'm all right," he said evenly. "Whatever made you think that I wasn't?"

Miss Eells said nothing, but the puckered frown on

her face told Anthony that she was definitely wary.

Emerson's smile faded, and for an instant there was a flicker of irritation in his eyes. "I'm here to help," he said, "but I get the impression that I may not be wanted."

Again Miss Eells was at a loss for words. She began to stammer, and tears sprang to her eyes. "Oh, no, Em, not . . . not at all! I'm awfully glad to see you, but . . . but, well, you seem sort of odd."

Emerson laughed. "Odd? I'm just trying hard to be calm, which I gather is not the correct thing to be doing right now. But we're wasting time, aren't we? It's clear that you were going somewhere and that you've had an accident. Were you on your way up to see me?"

There were a few tense moments while Miss Eells seemed to be debating with herself. Finally she spoke. "We're going up to Duluth, Em, and we need a ride badly. Can you drive us?"

Anthony gasped. Miss Eells was taking a chance, and he felt in his heart that she was wrong. But she was older and wiser than he, and Emerson was her brother. Maybe it would work out.

Emerson looked strangely surprised. "Duluth? Why do you want to go there?"

"Never mind. It's . . . it's private business. But the question is, will you drive us? If you won't, I can rent—"

Emerson cut her off with a wave of his hand. "Nonsense! I won't hear of it! If you don't choose to tell me why you're going to a ridiculous place like Duluth at this time of year . . . well, I suppose you don't have to. My car's outside, so if you will just finish what you're doing, we can go. But we'd better hurry—there's a storm brewing, you know."

Miss Eells hesitated again. Then she turned to Mr. Johnson, who had been watching the two of them. On his face was his normal look of dopey amusement.

"I guess I won't be needing your car-rental service after all," said Miss Eells half-apologetically. "So if you'll tell me what the towing bill is, I'll pay it and we'll be on our way."

After Miss Eells had written Mr. Johnson a check, she sent Anthony out to the Dodge to bring back the tool bag. Then they followed Emerson out of the garage and down the street. There, parked by the curb, was Emerson's car. He drove a 1938 La Salle, the big, bulky old-fashioned luxury sedan with the high metal grille and teardrop-shaped headlights. Miss Eells smiled when she saw the old car. Somehow it seemed reassuring—a reminder that Emerson was still the same person he always had been. When the tool bag had been stowed in the trunk, Anthony climbed into the backseat, and Miss Eells got in front with her brother.

They drove for miles. Snow was still falling, but the road had been plowed, so it was not as slippery as it had been. However, it was obvious that the weather was going to get worse. Behind them, to the south, the sky was black, and the wind seemed to be getting stronger.

Hard gusts hit the car, making it sway and shudder. Anthony peered out of the windows, but all he could see was trees and snowy fields.

It was really getting dark now. Anthony took his pen-lite out of his pocket and played the beam on the face of his watch. 4:15. He wondered how long it would take to get to Duluth. Miss Eells had reserved a room at the Hotel Duluth, and they planned to check in before driving to the cemetery. But the accident had messed up their plans, and this storm was going to mess them up even more. Anthony sighed and began to imagine the hotel room: flowered wallpaper, a warm bed with a blue fuzzy blanket, a table with a lamp and . . . Suddenly Anthony stopped daydreaming. A disturbing thought had just occurred to him. The two people in the front seat had been silent since the beginning of the trip. Usually Miss Eells and Emerson talked like crazy to-gether. Anthony looked toward the motionless heads in front of him, and he was afraid.

Suddenly Emerson broke the silence. "Myra?"

"Yes, Em?" Miss Eells's voice sounded cold and a bit trembly.

"Why are you going up to Duluth? I really would like to know."

A pause. The motor purred on, and a gust of wind shook the car.

"I'd . . . I'd rather not tell you," said Miss Eells, in a strained, guarded voice.

"I see," said Emerson coldly. He paused again and then added, in an unpleasant, biting tone, "I must say it all seems strange to me. We're brother and sister, after all, and we're used to confiding in each other. So, why won't you tell me?"

Miss Eells took a deep breath and let it out. "Well, Em, if you must know," she said at last, "I haven't felt like trusting you lately. Ever since our visit to Anders Borkman's estate, you've been acting strange. I was wondering if he . . . well, maybe, hypnotized you. There! I've said it, and it's a relief to get *that* off my chest!"

Anthony sat up, tense and rigid, on the seat. His heart was pounding now. What would Emerson say? Would he be hurt, or angry, or worse? When Emerson spoke, his voice had a sly, mocking tone that chilled Anthony. "You don't know what kind of person Borkman is at all! You don't have the slightest, tiniest, idea. *And because you are ignorant and foolish, I say* WOE UNTO YOU! *May you perish from the surface of the earth!*"

Anthony's body grew rigid with terror. These last hateful words were spoken in a resonant voice that was not Emerson's. It was the voice of Anders Borkman. And as Anthony watched, the car slowed and Emerson's body began to dissolve, literally unravel into strands of gray smoke till it disappeared. Then the windshield and windows melted and ran, like water. The rest of the car turned to bluish-black smoke, and the seat Anthony was sitting on shriveled and dwindled until Anthony was dumped, with jarring, painful suddenness, on the hard snowy surface of the road. Miss Eells landed near him, and with a *clunk* the tool bag fell nearby. Suddenly they were alone, stranded on an empty highway in the black night, with a howling storm coming on.

CHAPTER TWELVE

Anthony sat there stunned. But after a few moments, the biting wind and the awful fear of this lonely cold place jolted him into action. He scrambled to his feet and looked around wildly. Miss Eells was sitting in the middle of the road, her arms folded on her knees, shaking her head. Carefully, with his hands under her armpits, Anthony began to ease her to her feet.

"Is Em dead?" she moaned. "What happened? Oh, my poor brother!" Miss Eells began to cry, letting out big, gulping sobs.

"It's okay," said Anthony soothingly. "We're alive, and . . . I don't think that was Emerson. It must've been some kind of a trick or a phantom. We have to find someplace where we can get out of this storm." Gently

Anthony took Miss Eells by the arm. He pointed off toward the swaying, blurry evergreen trees in the snowy field beyond the road. "Let's go look, okay?"

Miss Eells shivered and did up the snaps on her winter jacket. She had stopped crying and even managed a wry little grin. "Who knows?" she said, shrugging. "Maybe we'll find a sleigh and some horses."

Anthony picked up the satchel, and together he and Miss Eells started off across the snow-covered field. The wind whistled, and a sudden fierce blast made them both stagger sideways. With his free hand Anthony pulled his red leather cap down over his ears as far as it would go, and struggled on. But he had only taken a few steps when Miss Eells stopped him.

"Anthony, this is madness!" she yelled. "There isn't anything over there but wilderness! We'd better walk on the road and hope that somebody comes."

Anthony realized instantly that Miss Eells was right. They stood in the ankle-deep snow on the side of the empty, dark road and waited. Several long, dragging minutes passed. Miss Eells hung her head, and tears began to flow down her cheeks. "A-Anthony," she sobbed, "we . . . we're g-going to die! No one would be crazy enough to come out on a night like this. No . . ."

Miss Eells's voice trailed off. They stood dead still, listening. The sound of a motor rose above the roar of the wind. Now they saw headlights and a flashing yellow dome light. A bulky shadow materialized out of the gloom, and they could see what it was—a truck with a snowplow on the front. As they watched, the big curved yellow blade shot a plume of snow off to the right. Anthony jumped up and down and yelled. As the truck got nearer, the roar of its motor was deafening. The two travelers started to get out of the way, but the truck began to slow, and then it stopped. A window rolled down, and a familiar long face appeared. It was Mr. Johnson.

"Hi there!" he called. "You folks need a ride?"

Miss Eells and Anthony looked at each other in utter astonishment. Then, with a joyful yell and a wave of her hand, Miss Eells started forward. She climbed up into the truck and slid over to make room for Anthony. *Slam* went the door. They were inside, in the warm cab that smelled of pipe smoke and grease. Mr. Johnson was there, in his coveralls, a parka, and—as usual—his baseball cap. His straw-colored hair stuck out from under the bill of his cap, and the expression on his face was calm, as if he was used to picking up stranded people on lonely roads during snowstorms.

"Your ride leave you in the lurch, did he?" he asked.

"Yes," said Miss Eells, grinning from ear to ear. "We're *so* happy to see you! What on *earth* are you doing up in this neck of the woods?"

Mr. Johnson shrugged. "I was jist goin' t' plow some back roads. It's a long ways from Eau Claire, but I got friends up here, an' if I don't plow the roads for 'em, chances are nobody will. After I get finished with the plowin', I'm gonna go on up to Superior, to my sister's place, an' get a cuppa coffee. I heard you say you were goin' to Duluth. I c'n take you as far as Superior once I get done with my plowin'. How'd that be?"

Anthony's heart leaped. He had been looking at the road map in Miss Eells's car, and he knew that Superior, Wisconsin, was right next to Duluth. "How . . . how far are we from Superior?" he asked excitedly.

"Only jist a coupla miles, er, maybe three," said Mr. Johnson, pointing at the dark windshield.

For the last minute or so Miss Eells had been silent. But her mind was working furiously. Finally she spoke. "Mr. Johnson, we *have* to get to Duluth! We simply have to! We have a terrible emergency. I'm the sister of a nun who's up at St. Scholastica's College. She's dying, and I have to be with her. If you'll forget about your plowing and drive us straight up to St. Scholastica's, I'll give you a check for a hundred dollars. Will you do this for us? *Please?*"

Anthony held his breath. Would Mr. Johnson ever believe this tale?

For about half a minute, Mr. Johnson said nothing. He rubbed his chin and stared at the two of them. Then his eyes narrowed, and his mouth drew into a hard thin line. "That guy that picked you up at my garage—was he your brother?" he asked.

Miss Eells hesitated a second. Then, with an odd half-smile on her face, she said, "Yes, he was. Why?"

Mr. Johnson looked indignant. "Well, if that's the case, he's a real louse!" Mr. Johnson heaved a disgusted sigh and threw the truck into gear. It began to move forward down the road. "Look, lady," he said, "I dunno what's goin' on in your family, an' I don't wanta know. But I'm gonna take you up there to that college tonight, an' you can pay me what you feel like payin' me. Jist sit back 'n' enjoy the ride!"

Miss Eells and Anthony were ecstatic. According to what Miss Eells had said earlier, the college was near their destination, St. Boniface's Cemetery. Soon they would be there.

As the truck raced down the road Mr. Johnson sang "Yon Yonson" and offered them a Thermos full of hot coffee. As they drank the hot liquid Anthony reached out and turned on the radio. Through the waves of static they heard a frightened announcer talking about the wild storm that had come roaring north from the region around Hoosac. He told of strange glaring lights that had appeared in the sky and of rumblings deep down in the earth. People were panicking, and the National Guard had been called out to keep order in some towns. Although the announcer continued in his trembly, nervous voice, Miss Eells had heard enough; she leaned over and switched the radio off.

They rode on in silence. Outside the windows of the truck the snow swirled as flakes danced madly through the headlight beams. Far ahead was St. Boniface's Cemetery, and Anthony could not help but wonder what would be waiting for them there. Finally they saw the Duluth city-limits sign. In the dead of winter Duluth looked like a frozen, run-down San Francisco with its steep hills rising above the ice-locked harbor. They were riding down the main business street of the city, but there was no traffic at all. The streetlights burned brightly, and the cars parked along the curb looked like white, snowy humps. Mr. Johnson forced the truck forward, sending jets of snow over the already buried cars. "Snow's changed," he muttered. "Gettin' wetter. Windshield's icin' up."

"Oh, great," said Miss Eells. "Look, Mr. Johnson, we have to get up to the college as soon as we can. How far is it?"

Mr. Johnson pointed off to the left, toward the steep streets that ran up into the hills. "It's up there somewhere. Not sure which street's the best one t' take. So I guess we might's well try this one that's next. Hang on, everybody!"

Mr. Johnson braked at the intersection and paused. The street had been plowed recently, but it was covered with a white, slick, sparkling layer, and the truck swerved as it started up the hill. It went a few yards, but then it stalled. Mr. Johnson jammed down the accelerator, and the engine raced. From beneath the truck came a loud, futile whining. The wheels spun madly, and then slowly the tow truck began to roll backward. Swerving from side to side, it went careening back down through the intersection, leaped a curb, and with a loud reverberating boom flattened a mailbox and came to a halt against the side of an office building.

CHAPTER THIRTEEN

Anthony checked his arms and legs—to his surprise he was not hurt. Then Mr. Johnson spoke.

"That was dumb of me!" He groaned. "I shoulda had my brakes checked! Boy, was I dumb!"

Miss Eells wrinkled up her nose and shook her head. "I think I've read this script before," she said sourly. "Between your bad brakes and my half-bald, chainless tires we make a great pair. I think we're all lucky to be alive."

Anthony looked out at the snowy, windy night and saw a traffic light swaying wildly on its thick, black wire. Snow gusted around the dark buildings. All the stores were closed up, and there was no one to be seen anywhere. Anthony's heart sank. How were they ever going to get to the cemetery now? He wondered if Borkman had iced the streets just to keep them from getting there.

Miss Eells started to talk, but her voice trailed off. She had seen and heard something outside. Now Anthony and Mr. Johnson heard it, a rising roar. Into the deserted intersection crawled a U. S. Army weapons carrier, a strange-looking contraption that was made to move around in the worst possible weather. It had been repainted in the blue and white colors of the Duluth Police Department, and it looked like a tank with its top half sawed off. Instead of wheels it had a rotating cleated belt, and in the driver's seat was a policeman wearing a helmet and goggles. As they watched, the weapons carrier turned slightly and began crawling toward them. It stopped in front of the truck, and the policeman vaulted down from his seat.

"Uh, oh. Now we're gonna get it!" said Mr. Johnson as he rolled his window down.

The policeman stopped below the window and glared up. In his gloved hands were a pencil and a ticket pad. "Gonna hafta ticket ya, friend!" he growled. "Know it's bad weather, but ya still shoulda had more control over yer vee-hickle. Yer from Wisconsin. What're you'n yer truck doin' around here, anyway? They call you in to help plow the streets?"

Mr. Johnson was just about to answer, when Miss Eells cut in quickly. "Officer, this gentleman was on an errand of mercy. You see, our car broke down on the way to Duluth, and he gave us a ride. We'd have frozen to death out in the wilderness if it hadn't been for him."

The policeman looked at Miss Eells. His eyes were hidden by the shiny polarized goggles, but his mouth was curved into a skeptical scowl. "Oh, yeah? Well, that was real nice of him, wasn't it? And may I ask where the heck *you* were goin' in this storm?"

Miss Eells struggled to keep her self-control. "Officer," she said in a polite, sugary voice, "I am the sister of one of the nuns at St. Scholastica's College. She is dying, and I want to be with her. My nephew and I have been invited to spend the night at the college. Mr. Johnson was trying to take us there when his truck had an accident. Do you suppose you could take us?"

Anthony gave Miss Eells an amused sidelong glance. He had seen her do her imitation of a sweet, helpless little old lady before and always enjoyed it. But would the cop fall for her line?

The policeman took off his helmet. He did not look quite so grim and forbidding without it. "Look, lady," he said almost apologetically now, "we're in the middle of one of the weirdest storms I ever saw in my life. People're scared half outa their wits, and I don't blame 'em. I hafta go up and down Main Street in this thing here and make sure that cars get moved an' stores don't get broke into. St. Scholastica's is way up that way. How'm I gonna patrol down here an' take you up there, huh?"

Miss Eells gave the cop her most pleading, round-eyed gaze. "Officer, it really is terribly important. We haven't got *any* other way of getting there, and I'm sure that by now the sisters are *frantic* with worry! Please, please help us!"

The cop turned his helmet over in his hands and stared at his boots. Finally, with a deep, weary sigh, he jammed the helmet back onto his head and motioned for the three travelers to get out of the truck. "Okay, okay! I'll take you! But move it, will ya? I ain't got all night. I gotta get back on patrol."

Miss Eells was delighted—she had won this round at any rate. Anthony scrambled out of the truck, clinging tightly to his tool bag, and she slid out after him. They both rushed over to the weapons carrier and climbed in. Mr. Johnson came loping across the snow after them. "Guess this is where we say good-bye," he drawled. "I'm gonna get a room at the Hotel Duluth for the night. No sense in tryin' to get back to my sister's place in all this snow. Tomorrow mornin' I'm gonna see about gettin' this crate o' mine off that sidewalk."

"You're gonna see about it earlier'n that!" said the cop irritably. "When you get to the hotel, call up a towin' service and then meet me back here in . . . oh, I'd say about twenty minutes to a half an hour. We'll get the old heap movin' some way."

"Good-bye, Mr. Johnson," Miss Eells called out, and she waved and smiled gratefully. "Thank you so much for everything!"

"Yeah, good-bye," said Anthony, and he waved too. "You were a real good friend to us, Mr. Johnson! Thanks a lot!"

Mr. Johnson grinned in his dopey way and ambled off into the darkness. The cop clambered up into the cockpit of the weapons carrier and started the engine. With a clattering of gears the heavy tanklike vehicle began to move up the steep, icy streets. No one was outside, though the streetlights burned brightly and many windows glowed yellow in the dark. The wind whipped around the weapons carrier, and it stung Anthony's face. But the snow had let up. Anthony wondered if Borkman's magic had run out of steam. Or was it possible that he and Miss Eells were wrong—was this just a natural storm that had nothing to do with Anders Borkman and the four weird statues?

The weapons carrier crawled up more ice-coated streets toward the highest hill above the town, where St. Scholastica's College is located. Looming out of the darkness Anthony saw big stone buildings with iron crosses perched on snow-covered roofs. The tall tower of a church rose into the dark sky. The vehicle rattled up a long, curving drive and stopped in front of a small pillared porch. Inside the vaulted roof a wrought-iron lantern with yellow glass panes hung, casting a pool of light over the snowy sidewalk. Anthony's heart beat faster. If somebody came out to see who was at the door, the cop would discover that Miss Eells had been lying to him. He glanced quickly at his friend and saw that her face was perfectly calm and composed. What a great poker player Miss Eells would have made.

"Well, here y'are," said the cop grumpily. "Don't say I never did anything for ya."

Anthony swung himself over the side of the weapons carrier. Nimbly he picked his way down the iron rungs and jumped off onto the ground with Miss Eells following, more slowly. Leaning down, the cop handed the tool bag to Anthony.

"Whatcha got in there, anyway?" the cop asked with a grin. "Scrap iron? Old horse collars?"

Miss Eells was flustered, but she managed to make a reply. "It's . . . it's a couple of holy statues and a sick-call kit that used to belong to my late brother, who was a priest. We wanted to use them when Father Flaherty administers the last rites to my sister. We . . . we had some trouble packing them on top of our clothes. They do make a noise, don't they?"

The cop stared at Miss Eells for a second. Then he laughed, waved good-bye, and the weapons carrier roared off. Miss Eells heaved a deep, heartfelt sigh of relief.

"My *Lord*!" she exclaimed, shaking her head. "I *never* thought he'd go away."

Anthony gazed at her admiringly. "You did great!" he said, beaming.

Miss Eells smiled. "Let's move out of the light and get our bearings," she said. "We need to find out where that stupid cemetery is, and I'd rather not be here when some nun comes barging out the front door to ask us what we want."

They stopped at a corner of the building, where some light was pouring out of a window above their heads. Here they were sheltered from the wind by a small grove of cypress trees that grew next to the building. Anthony took out his penlite and Miss Eells unbuttoned a pocket of her parka and dug out a wrinkled map of the buildings and grounds of St. Scholastica's College, which she had stolen from the Hoosac library. "The cemetery is off that way," she whispered, pointing into the blackness. "It's right at the northern edge of the college grounds. There's a hill to go down and another to climb to get to the cemetery. Come on. I want to get into that mausoleum and find . . . whatever it is that we're supposed to find."

Miss Eells and Anthony picked their way down the dark drive. The snow was ankle-deep and hard to walk in, but they plodded doggedly on.

"Down this way!" Miss Eells hissed as she grabbed Anthony's arm. "Be careful. I don't know how steep this hill is, but it'll be slippery."

Miss Eells unzipped the top of the tool bag and, after fumbling a bit, pulled out the flashlight. All around them now was pitch blackness. She played the beam of it on the ground, and they saw that they were standing at the edge of a hill that dropped off sharply. Anthony stood staring down, and he swallowed hard. He would have to dig his heels in and throw his weight backward, but he figured he could make it. But how was Miss Eells going to manage? Shuffling cautiously to the edge, Anthony took one step—and then he was gone. With a loud yell he disappeared into the darkness.

Terrified, Miss Eells rushed to the edge and pointed her flashlight beam down. Then she laughed with relief. Anthony was sitting there with his legs splayed out in front of him. His red leather cap had slipped down over one eye, and he seemed a bit dazed, but otherwise okay.

"Are you all in one piece, Tony?" Miss Eells called.

"I . . . I guess so. Only I don't know how you're gonna get down here. There's ice over the top of the snow, and it's real hard."

Miss Eells dropped to her knees, reached out, and tapped the icy surface with the butt of the flashlight. Yes, it was as smooth as glass. She stood up, picked up the tool bag, and gave it a heave over the edge. Then, with a brave smile on her face, she took off her glasses, put them in a pocket of her parka, and set the flashlight down on the ground. She nudged it with her foot and watched it roll down the hill, still lit and sending out a long, wobbly beam. Now Miss Eells lay down on her side and gave herself a heave. Over and over she went, down the icy hillside.

It was so dark at the bottom that Anthony could not see where she had landed. But then he heard a loud, cheerful exclamation.

"Well! That was fun, wasn't it? Now, where is that flash—ah! Here it is."

They scrambled to their feet, found the tool bag, and started across the slippery, ice-covered snow. Ahead was a flight of icy stone steps that rose into the night.

Miss Eells played the flashlight beam before them as they carefully climbed. Finally they reached the top. A low stone wall with a stone arch surrounded the cemetery. Atop the arch was a statue of St. Boniface, dressed as a bishop. Icicles hung from his crosier and outstretched hand. There was a wrought-iron gate, but no padlock.

Miss Eells and Anthony shoved the gate open and walked forward through the glimmering tombstones. At the top of a slight rise stood the Borkman mausoleum, a gloomy granite house with tiny slitlike windows. Two marble sphinxes crouched in front of the mausoleum, and two Egyptian pillars with lotus capitals held up the massive carved cornice. In the center of the cornice was a carved hourglass with wings, and above it the name BORKMAN. Between the pillars were bronze doors, which had tarnished to a bright green color. On the doors, sculpted in relief, were the upside-down torches that the article had mentioned.

"So, here we are," said Miss Eells softly. She could not hide the tremor in her voice. "I've never desecrated a tomb before. What do you suppose we'll find inside?"

Anthony said nothing. He looked around nervously. The tombstones were like small white creatures crouched in the darkness peering at him. The wind had died, and everything lay still. He could hear the blood roaring in his ears, and he felt his hands tremble; he was scared half out of his wits.

Silently the two moved forward. Anthony set the tool bag down in front of the mausoleum. Then, while Miss Eells held the flashlight, he took a long crowbar and inserted the curved, forked tip into the crack between the two doors. At first nothing happened, but Anthony kept prying, and soon the metal shrieked and groaned. Anthony struggled as he worked the end of the crowbar deeper into the crack. He stiffened his back, planted his feet, and shoved mightily. Finally the metal gave way with a loud crack like a pistol shot, and one of the doors flew outward.

Anthony stepped back. He half expected that shadowy arms would reach out and drag him inside. But nothing happened. Inside the tomb it was dark and still. From the half-ajar door a musty smell drifted out. Miss Eells walked forward, moving the flashlight beam around the opening as Anthony crowded in next to her to look. They saw a tiled wall and a terrazzo pavement decorated in spirally patterns. Overhead, from the vaulted stone ceiling, hung a rusty iron lantern with a burnt-out light bulb in its socket. But there was no coffin. It was totally empty.

CHAPTER FOURTEEN

Anthony's heart sank. He looked around the dark, gloomy chamber, and he wanted to scream. They had come up here looking for some unknown weapon that they could use against Anders Borkman, but there was nothing here, nothing but four walls, a ceiling, and a floor.

"This place is *empty*!" Anthony yelled, and his voice echoed weirdly from the vaulted ceiling. "It was just a lousy, rotten *trick*!"

Miss Eells laid her hand gently on Anthony's arm. "Calm down. Borkman is buried here—somewhere—at least that's what the old guidebook says, and they hardly ever lie. And I'll bet when we find Borkman, we'll find whatever it is we're looking for. In the coffin or not far away from it. Remember, the guidebook did mention some kind of fancy tomb-sealing device. So before we give up, let's examine this place carefully and see what we can find out. Okay?"

Anthony nodded wearily. "Okay, Miss Eells," he said. "You take the flashlight and I'll use my penlite, and we'll explore the whole place." Anthony's voice sounded dull and dispirited. He really didn't think they were going to find anything but dust and emptiness.

Miss Eells went over to one of the walls of the tomb chamber and began moving her flashlight beam around. Anthony got down on his hands and knees and began examining the terrazzo floor, which was made of concrete with lots of tiny marble chips set in it. The multicolored patterns on the floor were mostly whorls and spirals, but interspersed were other designs: a star of David, a compass rosette, a pointing hand. Anthony wondered if these symbols meant anything.

"Hey, Miss Eells!" he called out suddenly. "Come on over here, quick! I think I found something!"

Miss Eells started to laugh. "I was just about to ask *you* to come over here!"

Anthony got up and walked over to where she was standing. She moved the flashlight beam all around, and he saw that the wall was covered with small, square, shiny porcelain tiles. Most of these were plain white, like the tiles on a bathroom wall. But some had colored decorations on them: a rose, a gold-colored castle, a white tower against a black background, a silver star with long rays, and a gateway that seemed to be up in the clouds. Anthony also recognized the Ark of the Covenant from pictures in the family Bible. It was certainly an odd assortment.

"Interesting, eh?" said Miss Eells, tapping the wall with her hand. "Now tell me—do these pictures suggest anything to you?"

"Nope," he said, frowning in a puzzled way. "Not a thing."

"Well, they do to me. Remember that weird clue that ran, *There are openings in the choir of the Blessed Virgin?* My friend, this is the *answer*! You see, all those tiles up there—the ones with the pictures—fit into a prayer that Catholics used to say. It's called the litany of the Blessed Virgin. A litany is kind of a chant where the priest says one thing and the congregation in the church chimes in with a response. Well, in the litany of the Blessed Virgin the priest uses symbolic descriptions that are supposed to represent what the Blessed Virgin is like, and then the congregation responds with 'Pray for us!' 'Mystical rose . . . pray for us! Tower of ivory . . . pray for us!' And so on. Do you see?"

Anthony nodded. "Yeah, I guess so. But where does *that* get us?"

Miss Eells smiled and shrugged. "It may get us absolutely nowhere, or it may get us into the real tomb of J. K. Borkman. But before I go on, may I ask what *you* have found?"

Anthony pointed back toward the floor behind them.

"I . . . I found a crack in the floor. I mean, it's just a little thin line, but if you follow it all the way around, it's a rectangle. Like . . . a door."

"Ah-*hah*!" said Miss Eells triumphantly. "Here, hand me that tool bag. We are going to experiment."

Anthony was still completely bewildered, but he picked up the tool bag and handed it to her. She stuck her hand in and, after fumbling a bit, pulled out a screwdriver. Anthony pointed the flashlight at the tile with the rose on it, and Miss Eells began to pry at the edges of the tile. Almost immediately it started to move, and suddenly it flipped out. Not all the way out, because a long curved piece of steel was bolted to the back of it. Soon a sound like rolling marbles echoed from under the floor. Miss Eells grinned delightedly and rubbed her hands together. "Just as I thought!" She chortled. "There's some kind of elaborate pinball-type combination lock under this floor. And I have a feeling that if we pull these squares out in the wrong order, we'll screw the entire works up and *never* get the door open! Now, what comes after 'Mystical rose' in the—"

Miss Eells's speech was interrupted by a loud metallic *boom!* Instantly she and Anthony whirled around and looked toward the entrance of the tomb. The two bronze doors had been hurled inward by a mighty gust of wind, and they had slammed against the walls. Frightened, Anthony and Miss Eells rushed to the doorway and looked out. Several bolts of lightning crackled through the clouds above, and for a moment they could see the black silhouettes of distant buildings lit by a sudden bluish flash. Lightning crashed into a tree nearby and it burst into fire. A sulphurous, scorched smell filled the air. And, as Miss Eells and Anthony watched in horror, a blue ball of flame shot down out of the clouds, hitting the stone cornice over their heads and exploding into a million fiery points. They leaped back, and each grabbed a bronze door, shoving them together until they clanged shut. Miss Eells gasped as she stumbled away from the door. She shone the flashlight at Anthony. He was pale and sweating, and his eyes were as big as saucers.

"What . . ." was all Anthony could say. He was half out of his mind with fear.

"It's the final storm," said Miss Eells grimly. "But we can still stop him. Come on! There's no time to lose!" And seizing Anthony by the arm, she guided him back toward the tiled wall. Anthony pointed the flashlight at the pictured tiles. "After 'Mystical rose' comes 'Tower of ivory' . . . at least, I hope so," said Miss Eells, and boldly she picked up the screwdriver and began prying at the tile with the white tower on it. Again the clattering of steel balls sounded from below. "House of gold!" she panted, working feverishly. "Ark of the Covenant. Gate of Heaven. Morning star." And as all the tiles were flipped out, more noises rang out from below. Miss Eells and Anthony held their breath.

Then there was a creaking noise, and a section of the floor dropped slowly downward, as if it were swinging on unseen hinges. Below lay utter blackness.

"Well, what are you waiting for?" asked Miss Eells in a pretend-brave voice. "Let's see what the prize in the Cracker Jack box is."

They walked forward to the edge of the gaping hole. The flashlight beam swept down and showed a black wooden coffin that stood on two sawhorses. Six tall candlesticks stood guard, three on either side. Candles had once burned in their sockets, but now they were only messes of drippy brown wax. Miss Eells made the sign of the cross and muttered a prayer, but Anthony just stood and gaped, awestruck.

A howling gust of wind hit the bronze doors and rattled them. With a trembling hand Miss Eells grabbed Anthony's arm.

"Come on!" she croaked hoarsely. "We may not have a lot of time. If I'm right, the object of our search is inside the coffin with our dear departed friend. I know it's disgusting and scary, but we have to go down."

Anthony stared at the rough wooden ladder that led down to the tomb chamber. Picking up the tool bag, he pitched it into the room below, and while Miss Eells held the flashlight for him he started down. Then Miss Eells flipped the flashlight to him, and he held it as she climbed.

In utter silence they approached the coffin. A dusty brass plate with Borkman's name and the dates of his birth and death shone dully on its lid. They began to fumble at the edges of the lid, which projected out over the sides of the coffin like the lid on a grand piano. To

Anthony's great surprise it was not nailed shut. Still, as he seized the polished wooden slab with trembling fingers he was afraid to lift it.

Miss Eells was beside him, her voice quiet and reassuring. "I know we're both scared," she said, "but we can't come this far and then choke up. I'll count to three, and then we heave. Okay?"

Anthony nodded stiffly. The lid rose with a loud, grating *brr-rrr-rrrack!*, and Anthony involuntarily took a step backward. Unflinchingly Miss Eells pulled the flashlight from the pocket of her parka and pointed the beam in. There was J. K. Borkman, what was left of him, a skeleton in a rotting Sunday suit. Over the empty eyeholes perched rimless spectacles, and a knot of gray hair still clung to the dusty skull. His bony hands were folded over his chest, and the withered remains of a carnation were still scattered over one of the suit's sateen lapels. Anthony eyed the skeleton warily. He half expected it to come to life and leap at him. But it merely lay there, staring upward in grim repose.

Suddenly Anthony noticed something attached to Borkman's waistcoat. Strung between the slitlike pockets of the garment was a tarnished gold chain with a large, old-fashioned gold watch dangling from the end. But it was the crystal of the watch that fascinated Anthony; it had a crack in it that ran from the center of the dial up through the part of the glass that covered the number 12.

They had found the crack of noon.

"Miss Eells, look!" Anthony yelled, frantically stabbing his finger at the watch with the cracked crystal. "It's the crack of noon! It *has* to be!"

Miss Eells rushed forward. She handed the flashlight to Anthony, gripped the edge of the coffin, and peered in. "You're right! There's no doubt about it. Anthony, you're a genius."

Miss Eells reached out and picked up the watch. She held it gingerly and turned it around. Anthony was fascinated by the macabre scene, and he began to notice small details of the corpse that lay before him: the embroidered roses on the rotting, faded vest, the gilded elk's tooth that hung from one end of the watch chain, the bone that was missing from the ring finger of Borkman's left hand. *That's weird*, thought Anthony. *I wonder what happened to it?* He had an overpowering desire to reach out and rub his fingertips over the bony hand. He had never been near a real human skeleton before, and he wondered what the bones would feel like. . . .

Anthony's thoughts were interrupted by Miss Eells's voice: "Anthony," she said, "I want you to take the flashlight and go back to the tool bag. Inside it you'll find my purse, and somewhere there ought to be a nail file. Let's see if we can get the crystal off the top of this watch. And hurry, *please!*"

Without a word Anthony turned and started walking back into the darkness. He found the slouching leather satchel, and plunging his hand inside, he came up with Miss Eells's battered leather purse. In the midst of loose change, keys, coils of picture wire, plastic number puzzles, and inhalers, he dug out the nail file. Then he turned around and hurried back to her.

"Hold the light steady," she said when Anthony had handed her the file.

He did as he was told. The crystal was embedded in a gold rim that was fitted to the watchcase. A hairline crack showed where the two parts were joined. Holding the watch tightly in her left hand, she poked at the crack with the point of the file.

"The clue says *Pam under the crack of noon*," muttered Miss Eells as she struggled with the file. "I haven't the slightest idea what *pam* is, but it ought to be under here."

Anthony said nothing. He was becoming more and more jittery as the noises from outside—the muffled rumblings and the roar of wind—grew louder. Meanwhile Miss Eells was getting nowhere in her attempt to pry the watch open. Again and again she stabbed at the crack and tried to force the point of the file into it. But it couldn't be done. Anthony could feel blind panic rising inside him. But in spite of his fear he was seized again by the strange urge to reach out and put his hand on Borkman's finger bones. He wanted to touch the place where the missing finger bone had fitted to the rest of the hand. While he still held the flashlight steady in his left hand his right hand began to creep out toward the skeleton fingers.

Suddenly Miss Eells made a discovery. Dropping the file, she twisted the gold rim with her fingers. The rim began to move.

"It *unscrews*!" Miss Eells exclaimed. "What a nitwit I was!" With a few quick twists of the wrist Miss Eells had removed the crystal. Using the nail file, she began to pry the enameled face lose. While she worked on feverishly Anthony's hand crept forward.

After a few good twists Miss Eells had worked the watch's face free. She wrenched off the hands, ripped off the face, and peered underneath. Inside the body of the watch, instead of wheels and springs, she found a crumpled playing card—the jack of clubs.

"Anthony, look at this!" Miss Eells cried. But at that point Anthony's creeping hand had reached the finger with the missing joint. And when his finger touched the place where Borkman's lost finger bone had been, everything changed. The stone building rocked, as if it had been hit by the force of a powerful explosion. Anthony found that he was paralyzed, frozen in place, with his hand touching the skeleton fingers. Miss Eells couldn't move either but stood stiffly with the watch case in her hand. Her head was turned slightly, and she was staring at a figure that had suddenly appeared at the head of the coffin.

It was a man wrapped in a cloak so dazzlingly dark that it seemed to burn a hole in the gloomy blackness of the chamber. The face of the figure was lit by a wavering green light. It was a cruel, cold face with a heartless, mocking smile on its lips. It was the face of the creature called Anders Borkman.

CHAPTER FIFTEEN

"Who has dared to summon me in the midst of my most important work? Who has laid violent hands on the place from which I sprang?"

The green-lit face seemed to hover, bodiless, in the dark. Borkman looked from Miss Eells to Anthony and back again. In spite of the arrogant, mocking expression on his face he seemed strangely uncertain. But as he continued to gaze at Miss Eells his expression changed. The uncertainty vanished, and in its place came cold, venomous rage.

"You contemptible old hag!" he snarled, and he began to move toward her. "Haven't I given you an idea of what happens to those who try to interfere with my father's plans? I was called into being to complete my father's greatest design. And I have been faithful. The final spell is at work; the apocalyptic storm is loosed upon the world. Nothing can stop it. *Nothing!* But why in the midst of my incantations have I received a summons? *Answer me!*"

Miss Eells continued to stare, glassy-eyed. She held the watch case up before her, and the chain, pulled taut, was still hooked to the fabric of the dead man's vest. Anders Borkman raised his hand, and Miss Eells began to speak. Her voice was dreamy and lifeless, almost like a recording.

"We came here because of the clues in your father's diary. We hoped that we might find something that we could use to stop the storm you have started."

Anders Borkman laughed loudly, unpleasantly. "You really are a fool," he said, gazing steadily at Miss Eells. "My father had no desire to stop his plan from being carried out. He would never have left anything that would stop the storm. You have come up here for nothing. Give me the thing you have taken, and I will show you what a mistake you have made. *Give it to me! Now!*"

These last words were said in a harsh, commanding tone. Stiffly Miss Eells held out her hand, and Borkman grabbed the watch case from her. He glanced down at the crumpled playing card, and the uncertain look returned to his face. He seemed bewildered, almost as if he had never seen a playing card before. Now he reached out and plucked with his fingertips at the edge of the piece of stiff, crinkled cardboard. Slowly he eased it upward. Aha! Another surprise! There was something under the card. A small glass tube about two inches long. It was capped at both ends with silver, and there was raised lettering on the caps. Inside the glass was a dark reddish substance.

Borkman let the playing card drop. It fluttered to the floor. With his index finger and thumb he reached into the watch case and picked up the tube. . . .

And then something totally unexpected happened. Long shafts of red light shot out of the glass. Lurid rays jabbed in all directions, splashing bloody color over the walls and floor of the chamber and the staring skull of the corpse in the coffin. Still clutching the tube, Borkman dropped the watch case and staggered backward. He bumped into one of the tall candlesticks, and it fell over with a loud, echoing clatter. Then one sudden, dazzlingly strong beam flung upward from the tube. It was like a long, phosphorescent crimson spike, and it struck Anders Borkman full in the face. He screamed horribly, his red-lit face a mask of agony and terror. Then a blinding white flash, like a phosphorous bomb, went off in the room, followed by a dull *boom!* Miss Eells and Anthony fell to the floor. They were no longer paralyzed now—they were awake and aware and terrified out of their minds. They closed their eyes and covered their ears with their hands as flashes and explosions rocked the room.

Finally there was silence. Opening his eyes, Anthony peered out into the dark chamber. He could hardly see anything. Odd discs of pale red danced before him in the dazzling dark air. The flashlight lay nearby, and he groped until he found it and then turned it on.

Stumbling to his feet, Anthony played the beam around. J. K. Borkman still lay in his coffin, and Miss Eells was kneeling and crying with her hands over her face, but she did not seem to be hurt. Anthony looked toward the candlestick that had fallen. Near it lay a crumpled black cloak. And across the floor, in a twisting, snaky pattern, wound a trail of grayish-white dust.

Miss Eells took her hands away from her face and peered blearily about. "What . . . what on earth . . . ?" she muttered thickly. The steady beam of Anthony's flashlight still rested on the trail of dust, and suddenly Miss Eells understood. "*Dust thou art,*" she said in a solemn voice. "*And unto dust thou shalt return!*"

Anthony was still so shaken up that he was having trouble understanding what had happened. "He . . . he's dead, isn't he?" he said in a dull voice. "The . . . the widget in the watch case . . . it . . . it . . ."

"It finished him," said Miss Eells grimly. "He didn't think that anything in the world could stop him, but he was wrong. What in heaven's name do you suppose that tube was?"

"I dunno," said Anthony, looking around. "Maybe it's on the floor somewheres. Let's look and see."

They searched everywhere—under the folds of Anders Borkman's cloak, under the coffin, and in all the corners of the ugly old stone room. But the tube had vanished.

Miss Eells stood totally still, listening. Her eyes shone, and a triumphant grin spread over her face. "Anthony!" she exclaimed. "Listen, the wind has stopped. There's no thunder. The storm is over!"

Anthony and Miss Eells stared at each other in wonder for a few seconds. Then, silently, they began collecting their things, and slowly they climbed the ladder. On the doorstep of the mausoleum they paused to gaze at the scene before them. The ice-covered snow in the grave-yard had turned to slush, and a warm, springlike breeze was blowing. The sky was clearing fast. Stars were showing through torn holes in the clouds, and as Anthony and Miss Eells stood watching, the moon suddenly ap-peared, throwing a long silvery beam upon the statue of St. Boniface that stood on the arch at the entrance to the cemetery. His upraised hand seemed to bless the world and say that—after all the horrors—things were well again.

"Wow!" said Anthony softly. "We did it, didn't we?"

Miss Eells smiled wryly. "Well, *something* did it, that's for sure. Let's get out of this place." She paused and grinned. "Hmm . . . I wonder if those nuns over at St. Scholastica's would put us up for the night?"

Anthony and Miss Eells made their way down the stone steps that led to the valley below. It was easier going this time, because it was not icy, just wet. They went back to the building where the cop had left them, and, after pounding on the door a bit, managed to wake a nun, who let them in. Miss Eells told her that their car had gotten stalled in the storm, and wondered if they could stay the night. The nuns were very kind; they fixed a late supper of roast beef and potato salad, and gave them warm beds to sleep in.

The next morning the two travelers woke up early and slipped silently out of the building. They found a public phone booth, called a cab, and went to the Hotel Duluth. Since they had reserved a room there, Miss Eells figured that they might as well use it to take baths and figure out what to do next. In the lobby of the hotel they ran into Mr. Johnson.

"Hi there!" he said, waving. "How're you guys? Whatcha doin' here, huh? How's your sister? Is she any better?"

Miss Eells had to think fast. "She's, uh . . . fine. It was a false alarm. So we, uh, we thought we'd come down to the hotel here and not bother the nuns any longer. Oh, by the way, I owe you money for bringing us up here." She fumbled in her purse.

Mr. Johnson grinned. "Aw, forget it. I got my truck offa the sidewalk last night, only it's kinda bunged up. It'll hafta stay here in the shop for a while. So I rented a pickup. I'm gonna drive over an' see my sister in Superior this mornin' an' then I'm hittin' the road fer home. You guys like a ride back, wouldja?"

This was really too good to be true. Miss Eells smiled delightedly and said that yes, of course, they'd love to have a ride back, at least as far as Eau Claire. So off Mr.

Johnson went, cheerfully whistling "Yon Yonson." He would be back a little later to pick them up.

After he left, Miss Eells went to the front desk of the hotel and bought a newspaper so she could read about the storm. Then she and Anthony went to the dining room and gorged themselves on blueberry muffins, scrambled eggs, and coffee. Miss Eells was in a wonderful mood. She chattered a lot, spilled coffee, and read aloud the newspaper reports of the wild snowstorm that had raged across a large part of Minnesota and Wisconsin on the previous night. But Anthony was silent and moody. Now that the awful crisis was past, he focused on an immediate problem. In order to help Miss Eells, he had run away from home, and his mother was likely to set some kind of Olympic world's record for ranting and raving. What kind of punishment would she give him? Would he have to quit his job at the library? Would his parents drag Miss Eells into court and charge her with kidnapping? And amid all this brooding Anthony found himself thinking about Emerson Eells. What had happened to him? The ghost, or whatever it was that had pretended to be Emerson, was gone. But the real Emerson still had not materialized. Where was he? Anthony looked across at Miss Eells. She was buttering a piece of toast and leafing through the newspaper. She was not acting like somebody who was getting ready to put a black mourning band on her arm.

"Miss Eells," said Anthony suddenly, leaning across the table and poking his friend's arm.

"Yes, Anthony? What is it?"

"I was just wondering. I mean, what do you think happened to Emerson? We haven't seen him since he—"

Miss Eells cut Anthony off with a wave of her hand. She smiled knowingly. "If I were you, Tony, I wouldn't worry about Emerson. I think it's likely that Anders Borkman imprisoned him when we tried to invade his domain. Borkman had lots of chances to kill us back at the estate, but he didn't. I don't know why; maybe there was some rule that he couldn't kill anyone while achieving his grand goal. At any rate, now that Borkman is dead, all the knotted and twisted webs of sorcery that he wove will come untied. At least that is what I'm hoping. You see, Emerson explained this spell-casting business to me once. He said—"

A busboy appeared behind Miss Eells. "Is your name Myra Eells, ma'am?" he asked politely.

Miss Eells turned and looked at him. "Yes, it is. Why?"

"There's a phone call for you. You can take it at the front desk."

Miss Eells was startled for a second, but then she grinned and winked at Anthony. "Betcha a dollar it's Emerson," she said gaily, as she jumped up. "Betcha a hot fudge sundae at the Blue Moon ice cream stand."

Anthony shook his head. "No bet," he said.

A few minutes later Miss Eells was back. Breathlessly she reported that the call was indeed from Emerson. He was calling from her house, where she had left a note for him. He had been imprisoned at Weatherend ever since the day of the bungled break-in, but when Borkman was destroyed, Emerson found himself standing in front of the mansion. He took off running down the road and then heard this terrific explosion from the direction of the cedar grove. The four statues were being blown to glory. He made his way down to the gate and found his truck there. So, he just hopped in, started the motor, and zoomed off to Hoosac.

"Darnedest story I ever heard," said Miss Eells, shaking her head. "If I hadn't seen what I've seen in the last few months, I'd have called my dear sweet brother a liar." She sighed resignedly and sipped at her cold coffee. "He's waiting at my place, and do you know what he's doing to kill time while we drive back? He's going to clean my house! Says it's a filthy, unsanitary mess. Imagine—my own brother!"

After they had finished breakfast, Miss Eells went out to the front desk of the hotel to ask about the room she had reserved. It turned out that it had been given to someone else, who needed shelter from the storm. But that was okay with Miss Eells, since it meant that she didn't have to pay for it. Now there was nothing for her and Anthony to do but sit in the lobby and wait for Mr. Johnson to show up. They didn't have long to wait. Soon he came loping in, still whistling his favorite tune, and off they went in his pickup truck. When they got to Eau Claire, Miss Eells borrowed a car from him, and she and Anthony drove back to Hoosac. On the way home they put together a story about Anthony's disappearance. It went this way: Anthony had had an attack of amnesia, and he had wandered out of the house in the middle of the night. Somehow he caught a train to Minneapolis, and Miss Eells had run into him up there during the snowstorm while she was doing some Christmas shopping. He had been hiding in a hotel lobby, and he had seemed thoroughly confused. This was not terribly believable, but it was the best they could whip up on short notice. As it turned out, the story was gratefully accepted by his parents. His mother thought Anthony had left home because of the fight they had had, and she had been feeling guilty and worried ever since his disappearance. She was so glad to see him that she accepted this ridiculous story without any questions, and Anthony got lots of hugs and several big sloppy wet kisses. And of course his dad and Keith were very happy to see him home, safe and sound. So that problem was solved.

On the evening after his return Anthony got a phone call from Miss Eells. To his astonishment she told him that she had been reinstated at the library! When he had recovered from the shock, he asked her how that had happened.

"I'll tell you later," said Miss Eells smugly. "There are several secrets that need to be unraveled, and tales that need to be told. But first Emerson has got to go up to Minneapolis to do some research. So here's what we'll do: if the weather obliges us and turns cold again, we'll meet in three days' time and have an ice skating party on

Lake Hoosac. How about Saturday afternoon at two o'clock? Of course, I'll be seeing you before that at the library, but let's not talk about the reinstatement and all the other stuff you're wondering about. Ask me no questions until three days from now," she teased.

"Okay," said Anthony, and he went on talking with Miss Eells for some time. But he was in a state of shock. How, after what she had done, had she gotten herself back in? Well, he'd just have to be patient and wait for the answers to come.

Three days passed, and the weather turned cold again. Lake Hoosac had thawed after the storm, but three days of zero weather froze it right back up again. On the designated day Anthony arrived at Lake Hoosac with his skates slung over his back. Everyone was there, racing and whirring on steel skate blades. Near the snack bar stood Miss Eells and Emerson. Miss Eells was wearing her usual padded blue jacket and an old aviator's helmet with flaps that tied down under the chin. Emerson was clad in an immaculate powder-blue Alpine hooded jacket, perfectly creased gray trousers, and an enormously long scarf of blue and orange striped wool that was wrapped several times around his neck, the ends hanging almost to the ground. He wore no hat, but there were fuzzy blue earmuffs over his ears. The two of them had their skates on, and they were red-faced and sweating. Both were drinking cocoa from chipped china mugs, and they were looking very cheerful and relaxed.

"Hi, Anthony!" called Miss Eells, and she waved happily. "I've been skating for half an hour, and I only fell down three times. How about that, eh?"

Emerson stumbled forward on his skates and gave Anthony a hearty handshake. He looked a little tired around the eyes, but he had regained that bouncy, slightly arrogant air.

"Greetings, Anthony!" he said. "Myra's been telling me how you helped her, and I must say I always knew you were a tough, tenacious character. I'm proud of you."

Anthony hung his head shyly. "It's good to see you too, Mr. Eells," he mumbled, staring hard at the snowy ground.

Miss Eells tottered forward and kissed Anthony on the cheek, slopping the cocoa she had in her hand. "Oh, darn it all anyway!" she grumbled, looking down at the chocolaty hole that had been burned in the snow. "I ought to know better than to get emotional when I've got hot liquid in my hand. Anthony, we've got a thousand and one things to tell you. Why don't you wait here till Emerson and I get out of these skates, and then we'll all go sit on that old sleigh over there."

Anthony said that sounded fine and he waited for them. Then they all walked over to the dusty old antique sleigh that had been brought down to the lake to serve as a wintertime decoration. Miss Eells and Anthony got into the back, and Emerson climbed into the front seat.

"Well!" said Emerson, turning halfway round and peering owlishly at Anthony over his shoulder. "How does it feel to be a savior of the world? Eh?"

Anthony stared. *Savior of the world?* What on earth was Emerson talking about? "I didn't do anything to stop the storm. It just . . . sorta happened."

Emerson shook his head slowly. "No, my fine young friend, it did *not* just sorta happen! When you touched that place where the missing finger bone had been on J. K. Borkman's hand, Anders was summoned to the tomb chamber. He had to come—and when he did, he was destroyed."

Emerson smiled in a smug, infuriating, know-it-all way. "I can understand your being confused," he said. "I was confused myself at first. But I've done a little research in the last three days, and I think I understand it all now. In the first place Borkman knew you were going up to the cemetery. He was telepathic, and he could read other people's minds from far away. So he knew you were going up there to try to stop the storm. Naturally, he didn't want you to mess up his plans. So he sent the fake Emerson up there to track you down and dump you in the wilderness to die. Not that he was really *terribly* worried about you—he felt that he was invulnerable. And in many ways he was. If you had shot bullets at him or attacked him with a meat cleaver, he would have been totally unharmed."

Anthony gaped. "Really?"

"Yes, really. You see, Anders Borkman wasn't human.

He was a creature who had been created by old J. K. Borkman's sorceries. I know you'll find this hard to believe, but Anders was made from the old man's finger bone! He was supposed to finish the job that his creator had started. So he set up the four stones and began the magic rituals. He didn't think he had anything in this world to fear—but he was wrong. He had forgotten about the Blood of Hailes."

Miss Eells threw Anthony a sidelong glance, and she grinned. "Don't tell me you don't know what the Blood of Hailes is," she said sarcastically. "I thought *everybody* knew about that!"

"Well, everybody *should* know!" said Emerson, folding his arms and looking superior. "If children spent more time learning obscure facts and less time watching television, the world would be a better place. But I'm getting off the subject. The Blood of Hailes was a relic. It was owned by the Abbey of Hailes, in Gloucestershire, England. As I told you before, in the old days people venerated relics. Abbeys and churches actually owned things like the skull of Saint John the Evangelist or a bone from Saint Luke's forearm. But the Abbey of Hailes had a very special relic that had been given to it by the Duke of Cornwall in the year 1270. It was a small glass vial that contained some of the blood of Jesus."

Emerson paused dramatically and stared at Anthony, who was utterly flabbergasted. *"Really?"* he said again.

Emerson shrugged. "Who knows? It was an object with very great magical powers—of that I am certain.

And I am also fairly sure that J. K. Borkman thought the relic was authentic. I found his account of it in a collection of his private papers at the University of Minnesota. It seems that he bought it from a crooked antique dealer in a town not far from the ruins of Hailes Abbey. The Blood of Hailes was supposed to have disappeared when Henry VIII broke up the abbeys and monasteries back in the 1540's. Whatever the thing was, it's gone for good now. When Anders Borkman touched it, it was like what happens when you put hydrogen and oxygen in an electrolysis chamber—*blooey!* It's a shame, really, that the Blood of Hailes didn't survive. I'd have loved to hold it in my hands."

"Think you'd have been safe from it?" asked Miss Eells, in a needling tone. "Sure you wouldn't have gotten zapped, like old Uglypuss?"

Emerson snickered. *"My strength is as the strength of ten, because my heart is pure,"* he said. "Never fear, sister mine. I would not have gotten pulverized. Nor would you have. Even Mrs. Oxenstern, as unpleasant as she is, would have been safe. The Blood of Hailes—like most talismans—would only spring to life when it came in contact with a thoroughly evil force. In this case the evil force was so utterly, totally demonic that the two destroyed each other."

Anthony stirred in his seat and wrinkled up his forehead. As far as he was concerned, there was still a lot in this business that didn't make sense. "Mr. Eells," he said hesitantly, "how come old Borkman left the tube behind?

I mean, if he really wanted his plan to succeed, [...] he have smashed it with a hammer or something? He even left clues about how to find the tube. Why would he do a thing like that?"

Emerson lit a cigar and blew smoke out into the frosty air. "Interesting question," he said as he smoked. "The human mind is an odd, contradictory thing, Anthony, and people are capable of holding two opposite views at the same time. With one half of his mind old Borkman must've wanted his miserable scheme to work. But there must've been a part of him—the nicer, more human part—that *didn't* want the plan to be set in motion. So that part of his mind made sure that a counterspell would be left behind, together with clues leading to its discovery."

"I'm glad," said Miss Eells soberly, "that I'll be going back to a thoroughly normal world of overdue books and kids yelling and throwing spit wads in the East Reading Room. Even Charley Petersen and his windup teeth will be a treat after Anders Borkman!"

With a shock it came back to Anthony that Miss Eells was not going to be fired after all.

"I'll bet you're wondering what sort of double-dealing and skullduggery we pulled to get Myra back in at the library, aren't you?" said Emerson, his eyes twinkling with suppressed amusement. "Well, friend, as strange as it may seem, the whole thing was perfectly legal. You see, after Myra did her little dance act up in the Genealogy Room that day, she assumed—indeed, *everyone*

...ed—that there must be a clause in her contract that would allow the Library Board to fire her. But Myra's contract was drawn up years and years ago by old Mrs. Lesh, the former head librarian. Mrs. Lesh adored Myra, and she also knew that Myra was stubborn, cranky, and independent. So when she gave Myra her long-term contract, she put in a clause that said that she could not be fired *for any reason*. Myra hadn't read her contract carefully for years, so she had forgotten about that cute little clause. Anyway, if Myra wants to put on a pink leotard and go dance on the roof of the library, she can do it. Her job is secure until the day she retires, or until she dies."

Anthony was amazed, and he was delighted too. "Gee, Miss Eells, that's great!" he said, grinning from ear to ear. "I'm so glad! Is it true?"

Miss Eells smiled placidly. "Of course, I will have to put up with some unpleasant stares and hateful, back-biting remarks when I go back to work, but at my age I could care less what the dowagers on the Library Board think. And I have to admit that the whole thing has its funny side. I mean, I would never, *ever* have done anything disgraceful like that if I hadn't been under a spell, but be that as it may . . . Well, I keep thinking of the way Mrs. Oxenstern looked when I dumped punch all over her. It was really a pretty rare scene."

"Rare indeed," sniffed Emerson. He looked discontentedly around, and then he shivered violently. *"Brrrh!"* he said, hunching up his shoulders and hugging himself.

"It really is cold out here. Why don't we all go back Myra's place for a game of Scrabble and some hot buttered rum?"

Anthony and Miss Eells agreed happily, and the three of them climbed down from the sleigh and began crunching across the snow toward Miss Eells's car. Emerson had bought her a brand-new Cadillac to replace the Dodge. As they walked it suddenly occurred to Anthony that one last thread had been left hanging. He still didn't know what *pam* meant.

When he asked about it, Emerson chuckled. "Funny you should mention it," he said, "just as we are going off to embroil ourselves in a nice cutthroat game of Scrabble. It seems that there is an old eighteenth-century card game called *loo*. And in this game there's a trump card called *pam*. It happens to be the jack of clubs. Does that make everything clear?"

"You're becoming an expert on everything in your old age," said Miss Eells as they reached the car.

Emerson bent over and began unlocking one of the doors. "Now, I hope you're not criticizing, Myra," he said. "I could add a word or two about you. People tend to think of librarians as fussy, meticulous types, but after seeing your housekeeping and listening to some of the things you say, I have often wondered how you managed to get a job like—*aaah!*"

Emerson straightened up suddenly and grabbed at the back of his neck. During his little speech he had had his back to the other two, and so he had not noticed Miss

...us sneaking up on him with a lump of snow. With a sudden, swift motion she had stuffed the snow down the back of his neck. With a vengeful roar Emerson whirled and stooped. Hurriedly he made a snowball, and as his sister retreated toward the trees he let it fly. Miss Eells ducked, and the snowball flew over her head. There was a loud *whap* as the snowball hit someone who had just rounded a curve in the walk that led from the lake to the street. Miss Eells and Anthony and Emerson stared for a second, and then they broke up in uproarious laughter.

It was Mrs. Oxenstern, of course.

ABOUT THE AUTHOR

JOHN BELLAIRS is the critically acclaimed, best-selling author of several gothic novels, including *The House with a Clock in Its Walls; The Figure in the Shadows; The Letter, the Witch, and the Ring; The Curse of the Blue Figurine; The Treasure of Alpheus Winterborn;* and *The Mummy, the Will, and the Crypt,* which was a *School Library Journal* Best Book of the Year. Mr. Bellairs has also written a number of adult novels, among them *The Face in the Frost.*

A resident of Haverhill, Massachusetts, Mr. Bellairs is currently at work on another scary tale.

☐ **BONES ON BLACK**   15596/$2.75
SPRUCE MOUNTAIN
by David Budbill
Thirteen-year-olds Danny and Seth set out to explore Black
Spruce Mountain because they love camping out. But
Black Spruce Mountain appears to be haunted and their
adventure is more than they bargained for.

☐ **SNOWSHOE TREK TO**   15469/$2.25
OTTER RIVER
by David Budbill
David and Seth have a lot in common besides their age.
They share a love of adventure and specifically, they share
a love of camping and exploring. And what better place to
explore than the backwoods of Vermont?

☐ **CHRISTOPHER**   15599/$2.50
by Richard M. Koff
On a dare from a friend, Christopher knocks on the door
of a haunted house. There he meets the "Headmaster"
who teaches him how to release the amazing powers of
his own mind.